T0417757

Ophelia

Queen of Denmark

JACKIE FRENCH

Ophelia

Queen of Denmark

Angus&Robertson
An imprint of HarperCollins*Publishers*

Angus&Robertson
An imprint of HarperCollins*Publishers*, Australia

First published in Australia in 2015
by HarperCollins*Publishers* Australia Pty Limited
ABN 36 009 913 517
harpercollins.com.au

Copyright © Jackie French and E French 2015

HarperCollins*Publishers*
Level 13, 201 Elizabeth Street, Sydney NSW 2000, Australia
Unit D1, 63 Apollo Drive, Rosedale, Auckland 0632, New Zealand
A 53, Sector 57, Noida, UP, India
1 London Bridge Street, London SE1 9GF, United Kingdom
2 Bloor Street East, 20th floor, Toronto, Ontario M4W 1A8, Canada
195 Broadway, New York NY 10007, USA

National Library of Australia Cataloguing-in-Publication data:

French, Jackie, author.
  Ophelia : queen of Denmark / Jackie French.
  ISBN: 978 0 7322 9852 4 (paperback)
  ISBN: 978 1 4607 0192 8 (ebook)
  For ages 10+
  Ophelia (Fictitious character)—Juvenile fiction.
A823.3

Cover design by HarperCollins Design Studio
Cover images: Woman © Ayal Ardon / Arcangel Images;
all other images by shutterstock.com
Author photograph by Kelly Sturgiss
Typeset in 11/16pt Sabon Ltd Std by Kirby Jones
Printed and bound in Australia by McPherson's Printing Group
The papers used by HarperCollins in the manufacture of this book are a natural,
recyclable product made from wood grown in sustainable plantation forests.
The fibre source and manufacturing processes meet recognised international
environmental standards, and carry certification.

To Gillian Pauli, who gave us a Hamlet who breathed, sulked, and was also open to endless interpretations

With murder, ghosts, love, plots ...
and quite a lot of cheese.
And with apologies to Denmark and
its history.

Chapter 1

'You would be a good queen,' said the king's ghost, hovering above me as I sat on the battlements of the castle's tiny privy tower, nibbling my Wette Willie cheese. The tower's winding staircase was too narrow for watchmen in armour to climb up it, but ghosts and little girls don't take up much room. The wind tickled under my nightdress. It smelled of ships and privy and stubborn snow sitting on the mountains.

The king was grey mist, his beard and crown no thicker than a wisp of cloud. Beyond him, the farms and harbour's waves and forest were black under the blaze of stars. Down in the castle courtyard, torchlit shadows flickered. I wasn't scared of falling. At six years old, you don't worry about crashing down onto the cobblestones. I wasn't scared of ghosts either, though Nurse said they were fearsome visitors from the grave. But how could a ghost hurt me if it was just a mist?

And ghosts could fly! It must be fun to be dead, I thought. I'd tried to fly once, piling up the banqueting benches at our house and leaping off. But I just tore my skirt, and got a scolding from Nurse. She'd scold me now if she knew I'd crept out of bed, and through the door that led from our house to the castle, and up to the tower. And was talking to a ghost.

'What's it like being a queen?' I asked. I took another bite of cheese. Even at six years old I knew you only got Wette Willie for three weeks in early spring, when the lambs were frolicking and the ewes' udders were full of milk; weeks before the first cow's milk cheese was ready. In two weeks' time, the Wette Willie season would be finished for another year.

The ghost smiled. He had a nice smile. 'I was a king, not a queen.'

'But you had a queen,' I insisted.

'She died. When my son was born.'

'My mother died too.' I took another bite of the Wette Willie, then offered the remaining lump to him.

He shook his head. 'Ghosts cannot eat, child.'

'Not even cheese?'

'Not even cheese.'

I considered the matter. I was fond of cheese. I'd rather eat cheese than fly, I decided. Maybe it wasn't such a good idea to die. Or not yet.

'Is my mother a ghost too?' It hadn't occurred to me before that I might ever meet her.

The ghost smiled at me sadly. I could see the stars dimly through his face. 'If she is, I have not met her. Most people do not become ghosts. Only those who must walk the earth to avenge a wrong that was done to them become ghosts.'

'What wrong was done to you?'

The ghost stared out at the darkness that was Denmark. 'A man I thought was my friend got me drunk and tricked me into betting my kingdom on a sword fight. He won; I died. Now he rules my kingdom, and I must roam the world till I am avenged.'

'Oh.' That sounded like politics. My father talked politics. And talked. And talked. 'What does a queen do?'

'Sometimes she does nothing except let her ladies dress her, sew tapestries, and walk in her garden.'

That sounded as boring as what I was expected to do now. I wrinkled my nose.

'Or,' said the ghost, 'a queen can help her husband rule.' He gazed at me intently now, as if he wanted me to soak up every word. 'A queen can have power, if she has the courage to take it. If my queen had been alive, perhaps she would have stopped the fight. Perhaps, after my death, she would have led our army to fight the usurper who took my throne.' The ghost lifted off his crown and touched it gently, like it was a kitten and he a mother cat. 'Perhaps,' he said softly, 'she might even have won.'

I liked the idea of leading an army. On a white horse of my own, and dressed in gleaming armour, like my brother Laertes wore sometimes when he practised sword fighting. Girls weren't allowed to use swords … unless, I realised, they were a queen. A queen could fight

3

with a sword. Perhaps a queen could eat all the cheese she wanted, even before bedtime.

'Can queens do anything they want?'

'If they have courage and determination.' The ghost smiled at me again. 'Beauty helps too. People admire those who are beautiful.'

I nodded. I knew I was beautiful. Hair like wheat in the sunlight, my father said. Cheeks like a lily, declared Nurse. I knew I was courageous and determined too, but the ghost was the first person I'd met who seemed to think they were good qualities for a girl. Or for a queen.

'I'll be a queen when I grow up,' I decided. 'I'll fight a king and win a kingdom. I'll have to borrow Laertes's sword,' I added, 'and practise.'

The ghost looked amused. 'I am not sure you will find another king willing to bet his kingdom. Girls become queens by marrying a king, or a prince who will be king when his father dies. Or if their own father is a king who has no sons.'

My father was only lord chancellor, not a king. I must find a king to marry, or a prince. The only one I could think of was our Prince Hamlet. I didn't like him much. He had said I mustn't when he caught me climbing the apple tree. He was old, nearly fourteen, and was away now with his tutor in Wittenberg.

I'd have to find another prince. One who liked climbing trees. And cheese.

'Is your son a prince?' I asked hopefully.

'He is. But he has no kingdom to inherit. Not now.'

'Maybe he will fight our king and get your kingdom back?' Then I could marry him, I thought. And be the kind of queen who carries a sword and eats all the cheese she wants to.

The ghost looked at me seriously. He was the first person who had ever looked at me seriously, though of course he was a ghost and not a person, so maybe that didn't count. 'Perhaps my son may try to take this kingdom back. But I will not ask him to, not even to bring me to the gentle rest of death.'

'Why not?'

'Revenge is a dish that sits bitter in the stomach, even if the first taste is sweet.'

That sounded like Runny Roger: a winter cheese that was soaked in fermented whey, then wrapped in chestnut leaves. Runny Roger tasted good but gave you a tummy ache if you ate too much.

'Does that mean you will be a ghost forever?' I asked. There were no other girls my age at court, and it would be good to have the ghost to talk to. He was *interesting*.

'To be, or not to be? That is the question.' The ghost peered into the darkness again, as if he could see the beech trees, the cattle byres and pigsties of his lost kingdom. Perhaps he could. 'I do not know, child. Justice has a way of slipping into the world, like the sun creeping up into the dawn. One day, perhaps, my grandchildren will sit on Denmark's throne. But I will give my son his own road to ride, not chain him to my path with bonds of revenge.'

Rat droppings, I thought, borrowing Nurse's favourite

curse. I would need to find another prince to marry. I suspected there weren't a lot of them around. I swallowed the last of my Wette Willie regretfully. I'd hidden the hunk of cheese at breakfast time. Nurse didn't let me eat cheese at supper; she said it would give me bad dreams. A silly idea, I thought, sitting comfortably on the battlements with my ghost.

'Ophelia? Lady Ophelia? Drat the child. Ophelia!'

It was Nurse; she had tracked me down. A servant must have seen me come into the palace. Servants saw everything. I needed to get down the tower stairs before Nurse found me. The tower was my secret, even if my visits to the palace were not.

I slid off the battlements reluctantly. 'I have to go ... Your Majesty,' I added, remembering my lessons and sketching a curtsey.

I was still trying to think of a prince to marry. I wanted to ask the ghost if he knew of any, and how to make them want to marry me. And how to lead an army, and other things a queen might need to know.

'Ophelia!' I could hear Nurse opening and shutting doors below.

Tomorrow night, I thought.

'Goodnight, fair child,' said the ghost king. He smiled at me again, another sad smile, a strange look of hope upon his foggy face.

'Goodnight, King Fortinbras,' I said.

I would eat ten seasons of Wette Willies before I saw a dead king again.

Chapter 2

I stared at King Hamlet's body lying on the bed. His eyes were as glassy as those of the stuffed bear and wolf heads that gazed down at him from the walls. His face was blue, like polished wax. The servants had found his body lying in the garden, in the brief midday sunlight. They had carried him in here, but no warm bed or posset could help King Hamlet now.

Outside, the midwinter wind howled. Night had suffocated the brief candles of day. Ice-splintered waves slapped and sucked at the castle's stones. I envied the waves, free to crash and foam, while I was imprisoned in long skirts and polite manners as one of the queen's ladies, in a room that smelled of too many people, and a strange scent that must be death.

The queen stood next to me, her face expressionless as ice. With us were her other ladies: Lady Annika, crumbly as an old blue-vein cheese; Lady Anna, her grey moustache thicker than the hair on her head; and

Lady Hilda, round as a barrel of butter. They had been with the queen for most of her life.

The lords of the court stood behind us, silent in their furs and satin.

My father felt the king's wrist, then bent down solemnly to check he didn't breathe. 'The king is dead,' he proclaimed.

Of course he's dead, I thought, no one can be that colour and alive. But it was the proper thing to say. The sky could turn to goat's cheese and my father would still make sure his stockings were unwrinkled and the kingdom's accounts were neatly balanced in their ledgers.

The queen gave a small cry. Was it grief? I didn't think so. Surprise? But she must have known her husband was dead as soon as she saw him. She kneeled by the bed and kissed her dead king's cheek, then hid her face among the furs.

Lord Claudius, the dead king's older brother, put a comforting hand on her shoulder. Queen Gertrude took his hand in hers. He helped her up.

No one may touch a queen unasked, yet this man had, and the queen hadn't protested. I glanced at her, taking care not to stare. There were no tears in her eyes, nor on her face. Did anyone in this room weep for the dead king?

Father reached into his purse for two gold coins, then pressed the dead eyes shut, placing a coin on each to keep them closed. I waited for him to add, 'Long live the king.' That was proper too.

I had learned much about kings and kingdoms in the last ten years, through my reading in the palace library, and listening to Father talk at breakfast. Father should say, 'Long live King Hamlet,' and all the court must repeat the words. Prince Hamlet, son of Hamlet, must come home from Wittenberg at last and take his place upon the throne.

Instead, Father glanced at the queen, then at Lord Claudius. I waited for Lord Claudius to say, 'Long live King Hamlet!', for anyone at all to say the words.

The room was quiet as the dead king's breath.

Lord Claudius nodded to us, the queen's ladies. 'Take Her Majesty to her chamber.'

Still no one spoke. One of the minor lords coughed nervously.

Something was happening here that I didn't understand. The air felt as sharp as swords. Yet no man carried a sword here, in the king's chamber.

Queen Gertrude held her hands out to me. Soft hands, with sapphire rings and brown age spots; hands that had never done more work than hold a spoon or a needle. Yet this woman had the power to challenge my father about new taxes, and even sometimes to coax a kind ruling from the king.

'Lady Ophelia will come with me,' she murmured to Lady Annika, Lady Anna and Lady Hilda. 'Just you, my child.'

The others stood back to let me approach the queen, their skirts swishing silk against the bearskin rugs.

'Your Majesty.' I felt a thrill that she had chosen me, the youngest of her ladies. Her soft hands shook as I took them.

'Help me,' whispered the queen.

I put my arm around her shoulders, but as soon as I touched her, I knew she did not truly need my support. Her request was a message for the court. Queen Gertrude was saying as clearly as if she had shouted it from the battlements: 'This girl touches me as a daughter.'

The only way I could be her daughter was to marry her son. Who better to marry the new king, a stranger to the court, than the daughter of the lord chancellor?

My skin tingled. Next year, when the mourning period was over, I would be queen. I could have danced around the bedroom with one of the stuffed bears the old king had killed. My cramped, confined life as dutiful daughter and lady-in-waiting was almost over.

I had dreamed of the ghost's words ever since I had met him in the tower all those years ago. I *would* be a good queen. Other women were wives, nurses, tavern wenches, nuns, all obeying orders. A queen must know how a kingdom worked; she must understand the importance of fine weather in midsummer to make the hay to feed the cows over winter so they could give milk for cheese in spring.

My father knew how to tax the fleet that brought herring and stockfish, but Queen Gertrude knew why too high a tax on dried stockfish led to starvation. She knew when to give out soup to the poor in a hard winter;

how to ignore her husband's dalliances and cruelties; and how to persuade him — sometimes — with sweet whispers to put the good of the country before his games of hunting and bear-baiting. Queen Gertrude was the most interesting woman I knew.

I even almost loved her.

The best way to marry a prince, I had learned, was for his parents to approve of you. And to be rich and well-connected. I was all of these. And beautiful. King Fortinbras was right about that: kings and princes like beauty. And the continued support of the lord chancellor, the man with the largest estates and the most powerful private army in Denmark.

Of course the new king would need to agree with his mother's choice. But I could persuade Father to wear double stockings so his knees didn't ache in winter. I had coaxed old King Hamlet into sparing the young thief who had raided the palace larders midwinter; had made the old king laugh instead of having the boy whipped to bone and blood to amuse him. If I set my mind to it, I could set the wind to singing lullabies. I could even make Prince Hamlet climb an apple tree.

No, he was King Hamlet now. Young King Hamlet. I would make sure young King Hamlet was a better king than his father. Queen Gertrude had been a good queen. But I would be a better one.

Still there was no cry of 'Long live the king!' Were they waiting till the queen had left the room, out of respect for her new widowhood? I wanted to ask Father what was happening, but a daughter can only ask questions in the privacy of her father's house. And a lady-in-waiting waits.

I led the queen out of the stuffy room and the strange silence. She didn't speak, or even make a sound, as we trod down the cold stone corridor, ignoring the bows and curtseys of servants carefully hiding their curiosity. The old walls breathed out the scent of torch soot and damp.

We entered her chamber. The fire burned bright here, the wax candles smokeless.

'Bring warm wine and hot cheese with bread sopped in it,' I ordered.

The maid curtseyed and ran out, leaving us alone. I helped the queen onto the bed, slid her slippers off, then took her hand again. It felt cold, despite the fire, as limp as the hand of the dead king.

'I am so sorry, madam. I know you loved him.'

The queen hadn't loved him. She knew I knew it too. But a lady-in-waiting learns the polite words to say.

'I loved him not,' she whispered.

I met her eyes. Is that another reason I am here, I thought, and not your other ladies? Because I'm not shocked that you would say the words aloud?

Had anyone loved the old king? His mother maybe, once. Perhaps his son. But if Prince Hamlet loved the king, it was as a dream father. He hadn't seen the king in ten years. Nor had we seen Prince Hamlet. His home was among his friends and teachers and books far away down south in Wittenberg, not here in our cold stone castle, with icy waves, our forest and our cheese.

I thought of the king's corpse, lying between the satin draperies of his bed. He hadn't been a bad king, just a careless one. Old King Hamlet had loved his throne — so cunningly won from King Fortinbras — more than his people, or his wife. But he had left the kingdom alone enough to allow my father to keep it prosperous: the barns stocked with hay to feed the cows through winter; the cellars stocked with dried fish and sausages, butter and cheese. He had not objected — or perhaps not noticed — when my father consulted the queen, informally, as she sat with us sewing, about taxes or a new fishing fleet.

Suddenly the queen covered her face with her hands. She began to sob, deep dry cries that shook her body. She isn't weeping for the king's dead body, I thought. She is crying for all the years she had to spend with him alive.

She reached for me. I sat on the bed and wrapped my arms around her. I had never touched her before today, nor seen her touched, except when the king had casually kissed her hand at banquets. Even when we ladies dressed her, we made sure only cloth touched her skin, not our hands.

'Madam, do not worry. Please. Your son will be home soon.'

I wanted to add, 'Prince Hamlet will make a fine king,' but I didn't. The queen knew as well as I did that Prince Hamlet knew little about the land he was to rule.

Which was why he needed a queen who did. A girl who knew the court and all its gossip; who had heard about the affairs of state as her father pondered them each breakfast time, and listened to his discussions with the queen. Me. Ophelia. Queen of Denmark.

Queen Gertrude and I between us would ensure that every household had a dozen waxed wheels of cheese to feed them over winter, that enough hams and sausages dangled over the hearth to use as cudgels for the army if young Fortinbras invaded, as my father feared he would.

I would wear gold at my coronation, I decided. Gold to match my hair; gold for sunlight, for summer cheese, for butter. The sunbeams would dance for us.

But I couldn't say that now.

Queen Gertrude lifted her hands from her face. Her eyes were dry, her face anguished. 'Hamlet must not be king,' she whispered. 'Not yet.'

My dream cracked.

I stared at her. 'But he *is* king, madam.'

You didn't contradict a queen either. Shock made me bold. Hamlet had become king the moment his father ceased to breathe.

Queen Gertrude lifted herself up. I propped pillows behind her. 'My son has never ruled.' She seemed to speak to herself as much as to me. 'He hardly knows the kingdom. How can he be king?'

'But Prince Hamlet *is* king,' I said again.

'He will be king,' she corrected. She looked me full in the face. 'Denmark needs a strong leader. A man who can command an army. A man the lords know and will obey. Not in a year's time, but now.'

'You mean in case young Fortinbras invades, Your Majesty?'

Only this morning Father had received a letter describing the size of Fortinbras's army, marching near our borders. Fortinbras, son of the dead king whose ghost I had once talked to. Or had I? It seemed a dream now. Must have been a dream. Surely ghostly kings did not truly walk, nor little girls talk to them?

Young Fortinbras had not invaded Denmark — yet. An army could be put to many uses: its leader could hire it to a king, to keep order in his kingdom or to attack another. But the fact that Fortinbras had both a nearby army and a claim to Denmark's throne was worrying.

The queen's voice was firmer now. 'Fortinbras is less likely to attack if a strong king is on the throne.'

'But we … I mean you, and my father and the other advisers, can make Prince Hamlet strong, madam.'

'Not in time to stop an invading army. There is only one man who can be the leader we need now.'

For the first time the queen didn't meet my eyes. And all at once I knew.

I asked anyway. 'Who, Your Majesty?'

'The king's brother. Lord Claudius.'

'But Lord Claudius isn't even a prince.'

Just as his brother hadn't been a prince, or a king, until he'd won the kingdom in a drunken bet.

The queen looked at me steadily, as if she truly wished to see my reaction. 'No, Lord Claudius is not a prince. But he can be king if he marries a queen.'

I kept my face expressionless. One learned that at court too. So that was why no one had called out, 'Long live the king!' Others at court must have thought of this too.

'You would marry Lord Claudius for the sake of the kingdom, madam?'

The queen looked at her hands, at the wrinkles and age spots. Then back at me.

'I would marry Lord Claudius because I love him,' she whispered, as if the walls behind the tapestries had ears. Which, in a palace where gossip ran faster than fresh cream, they often did. 'I have loved him ever since I was brought to Elsinore to marry his brother. I had no choice then. But now ...'

Now you can have the man you want and still be queen, I thought. It would be hard to give up her seat by the throne to be simply the queen mother. And, I admitted reluctantly, the queen's decision might save the kingdom from attack. She was no fool, this queen of ours.

'Hamlet will still be king one day,' the queen added hurriedly, as if she wanted to convince herself as well as me. 'Claudius has no children. And I am too old to bear him one.'

How old was Lord Claudius? Sixty perhaps? An old man. But an old man could live for many years. And marry a young woman if his first wife died, who could bear children. Another insight I would not mention to Queen Gertrude.

'My lady, what will Prince Hamlet say to this?'

She lifted her chin. 'Prince Hamlet has no lands of his own, no army. There is nothing he can do. As for what he will say …' She met my eyes, then tapped me on the cheek. 'You must persuade him, my child. Tell him he will be king when he knows the kingdom well enough to rule it.'

And when King Claudius is finished with it, I thought. So this was another reason why the queen had sought me out alone.

I wondered how even a queen could know a man would want to marry her if she had not talked about it with him first. The king had died only today, and with no warning. Then I remembered Lord Claudius's face back there in the king's bedroom, how he had failed to say the words 'Long live the king'. Lord Claudius would not be surprised to be offered the throne tonight.

Perhaps he and the queen had even discussed what might happen one day, if the king were to die of plague or out hunting. 'What if he is gored by a boar?' the queen might ask, her eyes as calculating as a lizard's soaking up the sun's warmth.

Which was why I only almost loved her, for all she was as near as I had ever had to a mother.

But I admired her, as a queen.

'Yes, Your Majesty,' I said.

Chapter 3

The dead king lay in state for a sennight before the funeral, lying in ice in the palace chapel to keep his body fresh.

It was a week's travel from Wittenberg to Elsinore in summer, but now, in midwinter, drifts of snow blocked the roads, and ice winds kept ships from harbour. Prince Hamlet did not return in time for his father's funeral, nor for his mother's wedding three weeks after it.

The queen did not call me to her during the week the dead king lay in state. I did not expect it. She would spend the time secluded in mourning. She knew I had other duties too, beyond attending her. Unlike Lady Annika, Lady Hilda and Lady Anna, I did not live in the palace, but in my father's adjoining house.

Sometimes I wondered why Father had not moved to a palace apartment after my mother's death. Perhaps he had loved her too much to leave the rooms that she had furnished, the tapestries embroidered in her girlhood, her portrait in our hall. Or maybe he liked being lord of his own small kingdom each night.

I wore the keys of our household, and unlocked the larder each morning to give the cooks the day's saffron or cinnamon, Venetian almonds or Parisian chestnuts; and checked that the linen was aired, the cheese in the cellars turned regularly, and the brine in the barrels of salted butter changed each week. Ours were good cellars and I kept them well-stocked: three hundred cheeses, fresh and aged; five tons of salted butter; smoked sides of salmon, rows of hams and slabs of bacon; barrels of old brandy and new ale; crocks of honey; boxes of dried berries or hops; bunches of dried herbs hanging from the rafters — all sent from our estates.

But I helped to dress the queen on the morning of the king's funeral, in black lace, with a black lace veil across her face. I walked behind her, with her other ladies, wearing the black satin I'd inherited from my mother.

I helped to robe the queen for her wedding too. A widow wears black for a year after her husband's death, but black is bad luck for a bride. When I reached the queen's apartments, I saw the maids had laid out a new underdress of rich purple; purple satin sleeves, trimmed with ermine fur in black and white; and an overskirt of purple lace, trimmed with ermine too.

A good choice, I thought, as Lady Anna and I lifted up the petticoat. A widow moves from black to purple in her second year of mourning; and purple is royal too.

The maids sewed on the sleeves. Lady Annika woke up in time to drape the lace veil, and even smiled. If a withered winter apple smiled, it would look like Lady Annika.

Lady Hilda gestured with her small fat hands to the maids to bring the mirror over.

The queen stared at her image. 'Is that truly me?'

'It is, madam, and beautiful,' I said.

My father would have taken six pages to say the same. I had no taste for the long speeches of court. No one thought less of me for it. And it gave others an audience for their words.

The queen turned and smiled at us. She'd had us dress in shades of lavender; not bright, but not full mourning either.

'You are my flowers,' she said. She kissed me on the cheek. 'And you are the fairest flower of our court, dear child.'

The maids opened the door. We ladies-in-waiting held the queen's train above the stone floor of the corridor. Our own trains trailed behind. I would need to make sure my maid Gerda washed mine once the day was over. Castles breed dust, no matter how often they are swept; especially in winter, when soot from fires and torches and candles thicken the air.

The torches were lit along the corridor now, to hunt away the winter dark. The sun would rise only a handspan above the snow-lipped horizon today. Footmen opened the doors before us, down the stairs, across the great hall, through the receiving chamber to the chapel.

The chapel doors exhaled incense and perfumes and a faint scent of old closets. The guests stood: the women in grey silk and lace — we had been whispering the favoured colour for the past week; the palace women sewing, sewing, sewing, the dye vats bubbling — and the lords in grey satin. My brother, Laertes, his ship just back from Paris where he lived most of the year (and enjoyed himself too freely, my father feared), stood in the front next to Lord Claudius. He wore grey satin trimmed with lace and diamonds, and his hair was curled neatly. Laertes was almost a stranger to me, but I was glad to have a brother here, and a handsome one.

'Your Majesty.' My father bowed at the chapel doors. A lord chancellor did not give a queen away, like her father would have, but he preceded her up the aisle to the altar, giving the ceremony his blessing.

Father bowed to Lord Claudius, then took his place beside my brother.

The queen's eyes met her lord's. I saw her flush. I had not realised that women her age could love as the young do, until I saw it then.

Lord Claudius smiled. I tried to read his expression. Was it love? No, I thought. It is the look of a man who has played a game of chess and makes the final move to win.

The priest began to speak. And when the chapel doors opened again, Lord Claudius was king.

It was a fine banquet. Torches flared across the palace courtyard, driving away the afternoon shadows. Three oxen turned on spits, their dripping juices flaring in the cooking fires, for the townsfolk and ships' crews and any farmers who had travelled through the snow to join the celebrations. A cartload of barley bread was parked next to the fires, for them to eat with the meat, with barrels of ale, and minstrels paid to sing the new king's virtues. Laughter and music echoed up to the palace.

Inside the banquet hall, servants carried in whole roast boars with gilded tusks, venison with the deer's antlers also painted gold, and roast geese with berry sauce.

I glanced at the queen as the geese were set on the tables. Boar and venison were wild meats, but goose in midwinter meant we were eating birds that were being kept for spring.

I'd rather have had bread and cheese. And be *doing* something, even inspecting the linen for frayed edges, instead of hours of eating.

Still, a royal marriage feast did not happen often. The kingdom was prosperous. There would be enough geese left to lay eggs for goslings in spring. I ate my goose, my slices of boar, the almond custards dyed gold with saffron, and spiced almond cakes. And if the marzipan table centrepiece of the castle, towns and fields had been used three weeks before at the dead king's wake, stained black then and now covered with gold leaf, there was no one who would mention it openly.

Nor did anyone say aloud that if there must be a marriage, a quiet one was more fitting than this finery.

But perhaps the queen and her new king are right, I thought, as the next course was carried in: a whole stuffed pike with crabapple sauce; rose hep jellies; rows of gilded roast ducks and capons. This feast was to show that Claudius was king indeed.

The last sparks of afternoon sunlight wandered through the windows, lighting a jewel here, a silken headdress there, brighter than the torches. The fires roared deep red. The tables were dressed with gold and green and red: bread like golden sheaves of wheat, red marzipan cherries, green-painted apples. If my lady could not wear colours to her wedding, she had them all around her now.

The musicians played. No grey and lavender for them, but reds and greens too. I sat at the high table, with grey-haired friends of my father either side of me. Across from me, my brother flirted with Lady Hilda, showing all the charm he had brought back with him from Paris. I loved my brother with a sister's duty. When he winked at me, I suddenly realised that I liked him too.

More food, enough to stun an elephant: peacocks with gold feathers; roast swans with red-dyed apples. The lord of the exchequer passed me stewed figs with minced chicken, then carp in a mustard sauce. Lady Annika's eyes closed in a doze. If no one woke her, she would soon be face down in the lingonberry sauce. Lady Hilda's face glowed with goose grease, her cheeks red from too many pastries.

I glanced at the queen. She laughed as Lord Claudius offered her a leg of pheasant, whispering a joke into her ear.

Not Lord Claudius. The king.

Another tune. I wondered if there would be dancing. At a wedding, the bride led her ladies, but we had not prepared a set. A widow did not dance for a year at least. But then neither did she wed …

'Some hare, my Lady Ophelia?'

For a moment I thought the lord of the exchequer had said 'hair'. I stifled a giggle, for he had little hair to offer me.

'My lord, I thank you,' I began, then stopped.

The hall fell silent. The musicians lowered their tabors, mandolins and finger drums. Lady Annika woke, blinked, stared.

A young man strode through the hall between the tables. He wore black: black cloak, black boots, black feather in a black velvet cap — a crow among the grey silk doves of court. He was dressed for travel, not for feasting. Behind him came his attendants, less richly dressed than him, in deep black too. A mob of crows, come among the revellers.

Prince Hamlet. The man I had dreamed of marrying.

No, I admitted, I never dreamed of marrying this man. How could I when I hadn't seen him since he was a boy? I'd dreamed of marrying the prince. And here he was. Still a prince, not a king.

He looked … startled. No more than that. Perhaps he had been gone so long he thought Denmark mourned in grey and purple, not black, that the townsfolk sang and feasted every afternoon. He reached the middle of the room, then stopped and gazed around.

What is he waiting for? I wondered. And then I knew.

Prince Hamlet waited for the court to rise, to bow

or curtsey to the ground towards him, their new king. He waited for the trumpets to blow the royal entrance march, for men to cry, 'Long live the king!'

Surely the queen had sent messengers, I thought, to tell her son what she planned. Surely his uncle, Lord Claudius, had sent a letter ...

Or not. A prince warned that his kingdom was no longer his own might have brought an army home, like young Fortinbras, rather than the band of black-garbed servants we saw here.

My heart leaped out to him, his face white with travel and weariness, so alone in black among the silken greys. Of all the court, only Prince Hamlet did not know what had happened in the kingdom he had thought was his.

He stood there for perhaps ten heartbeats. And then he understood.

He gazed at the lords and ladies at the high table, at King Claudius, at his father's crown shining on his uncle's head, at his mother sitting at his uncle's side. He stood still and silent, as if the ice outside had claimed him for its own.

The queen stood and extended her hand. Her voice would have sounded welcoming and carefree to any who did not know her well. 'Hamlet, our son, and the sun of our winter lives. Your stepfather, the king, and I bid you welcome to your home.'

He did not take her hand. Nor did he draw closer. 'My stepfather, madam?'

'Your uncle, now your loving father.' For a pinprick of a moment the queen's voice held steel. 'And now your gracious lord.'

King Claudius stood. A more courteous host, or uncle, would have stood at once to welcome a nephew, now a son, home. He would have stepped forward to embrace him. Our new king had sat those long seconds to show Hamlet — and the court — that he could.

'A fond welcome to you, Prince Hamlet.' Was there a slight emphasis on the word 'prince'? 'We feel sorrow that you missed our wedding, but joy that you are here now to see our happiness.'

'Indeed, sir, I see too much, and all lit by your gracious presence too.'

Prince Hamlet looked around the room again. I held my breath. This was the time for the lords to rise and bow to him; to show they supported the old king's true heir and not the man who sat beside the queen. Surely some, at least, would stand for the true heir to the throne?

The room was silent. No one moved. Prince Hamlet had no supporters here. His every friend was at Wittenberg or standing, puzzled, behind him. Had his attendants also thought they were coming to their master's kingdom, with posts of glory promised to them? Prince Hamlet was what he had always been: a king's son. No, he was less now: a king's stepson. Prince Hamlet was a king's heir only if he kept the new king's favour. No more than that.

The queen let her arm drop. Her face was calm, but I knew the effort it took. 'You must be tired, my son.'

I could see the strength needed for Prince Hamlet too, to keep his voice steady. 'I expect to grow more tired of many things, madam, and quickly. If my welcome has been not as I expected, will you welcome my attendants at least?' He turned to his servants. 'Let my mother help you to her marriage feast. As her son, I will seek what sun there still is in Denmark while it may last.'

He strode between the tables and out the door. The cold air battered at the candle flames. The fires withered, then roared back.

For a moment I thought the queen would follow him. King Claudius grasped her wrist. She stood as still as the gravestone under which her dead husband lay, then forced herself to smile at Hamlet's servants.

'Kind gentlemen, I bid you, stand on no ceremony. Let your travel clothes be tokens of our joy that fate brought you here in time to share with us this feast.'

Already, lords were moving tactfully down their benches, making space for the new guests. They sat awkwardly. Servers placed trenchers in front of them and filled goblets. Mouths full of food can't argue for rebellion, I thought. Already one of the men was lifting a wing of pheasant to his mouth.

I glanced at the queen. In truth, I always watched her, as a lady-in-waiting should. Even when I had looked at Hamlet, I had been aware of her too. She nodded to me, so slight a movement that no one in the lower tables noticed. I stood and made my way up to the high-backed chairs where she sat with our new king.

I curtseyed, deeply. 'Your Majesties.' I let my voice linger on the plural.

'Go, find my son,' the queen murmured. 'If beauty can tame a beast ... well, you are beauty.' And sensible, said her look, if not her words.

'Yes, madam.'

Triumph rippled through me like a spring stream through the snow. Once again the queen had announced almost as openly as saying out loud: 'This is the girl I want my son to marry.'

But if I was ever to be a queen, I must tame an angry prince now.

Chapter 4

My father didn't notice as I slipped between the tables. Laertes did. Not much escaped this brother of mine, it seemed. His eyes narrowed as he watched me go, but he didn't rise to stop me. He must have seen the queen speak to me. One does not question the orders of a queen.

The corridor was empty, the lords and ladies all in the banquet hall, and most of the servants carrying food and drink up from the kitchens. I lifted my skirts so I could run. Once Prince Hamlet reached his chambers, I wouldn't be able to talk to him. Even Her Majesty would not command an unwed girl to be alone with a young man there.

A porter flung wood on the fire in the entrance hall. He looked at me, startled, and I saw a wine skin by his bench. He had expected a quiet time during the wedding and banquet.

'Have you seen Prince Hamlet?' I asked as he bowed to me.

'He and his attendants went to the banquet hall, my lady.'

'No, just now! By himself.'

The porter shook his head. 'No one else has been this way, my lady. Not a peacock nor a sausage, though if there had been a sausage, it would have been my supper.'

Fool, trying to ape the clever speech of his betters, I thought with half my mind. Or maybe not a fool. A clever porter might become a footman. Prince Hamlet must have gone through one of the doors I'd passed — to the library, or the music room, or up one of the smaller flights of stairs ... I stopped. I knew where the prince had gone. The royal garden, where his father, the king, had died.

The royal garden was the one place in the palace no one could follow him, except his mother, and the new king now, unless they gave permission for others to accompany them. The garden's walls gave privacy, except from the towers above. Royalty needs to be alone sometimes.

I had walked in the garden with Her Majesty while Lady Annika dozed on one of the stone seats. In summer, the garden was sweet with roses. In winter, the stone walls trapped the warmth. That must have been why the king had lain there the day he died, in the brief midday winter sun, more delicate than gold and a hundred times more precious.

But it was afternoon now, and the air was as grey and sombre as the silks of court. As Prince Hamlet's thoughts must be.

Did Prince Hamlet know his father had died in the garden? Poor prince, to lose a father and a kingdom and his trust in his mother in one short breath. The queen was right: her son needed comfort. But not from her, today.

I hesitated at the door to the garden. But the queen had told me to find her son. That must mean I had permission to enter her garden too.

I opened the door and looked outside. The sun hung low atop the garden walls, as if it was too tired to rise any further, waiting to drop as soon as possible into night. Snow had fallen while we were banqueting, and the paving stones, walls, grass and rose bushes were all so white in the last beams of light that they hurt the eye. The cold bit me like a winter wolf. I shivered in my silks.

I had been right. There was Prince Hamlet, his cloak black against the snow, standing at the far end of the garden, staring at the fountain, its water frozen glass.

I stared at him, this prince I had planned to marry. I hadn't had time to see beyond his loneliness, his shock and his anger before. He was taller than either his father or his uncle, but his shoulders were narrow — a scholar's physique, not a swordsman's like my brother's. He stood tall and straight, but he didn't look like a king, alone there among the bare thorns of winter's roses.

Shame bit me, hard. I had been dreaming about the position, without care for the man who held it, nor thought of his sorrow for his father's death and the humiliation he must feel now. A poor king with no kingdom, who must wait for his uncle to feed him a crown like scraps from the high table.

I must have made a sound. He turned. I curtseyed deep, as I would to the king or queen. 'Your Royal Highness?'

Prince Hamlet stared at me, his face twisted with anger. 'Not so high, it seems. Lower than majesty, benched with the courtiers, not enthroned. Oh, stand up,' he added, when he saw I wouldn't rise until he told me to.

I rose, wondering if he had any idea what it felt like to stay in a low curtsey wearing a tight bodice while a prince made a speech. 'Thank you, Your Highness. I am sent by your royal mother.'

He snorted. 'I did not think you had come to lead an army to my side. Not one man in that room had the courage or loyalty to stand with me, son of their great king.'

Not so great a king, I thought. A man who had won a kingdom with a bet; who had ruled it with so little love that both my father and his queen doubted that the people would fight for his son if Fortinbras invaded. Prince Hamlet's father's lack of greatness had led to this.

'My lord,' I said carefully, 'your day in the sun will come.'

'When summer comes?'

'You are still heir to the throne, my lord.'

'I was that a month ago.'

The snow was seeping into my silken slippers. I moved my feet back and forth under my dress to stop them freezing. I tried not to stare enviously at his boots. 'And you are still the heir, my lord. May I speak frankly?'

'What frankness can you offer me?' He looked at me as if I were a performing bear. 'Do you have honeyed phrases to woo me back to that farce they call a wedding feast? A thrifty man, my stepfather, the funeral leftovers furnishing his bridal banquet.'

'I would rather leave honey for the bees, my lord. I prefer to taste what is, rather than wasting sweetness to disguise bad butter.'

'Well, I have reason to be bitter. And I have no wish for honey. Speak, if you must.'

The sun dropped below the wall. Shadows claimed the garden now. Day's brief reign had ended.

I stepped towards him, trying to stop my teeth from chattering. 'My lord, they know you not. True, you have no friend at court, but no enemies either. Nor is the new king well-loved. Let the court come to know you, sir. A few months as the new king's heir, a few years perhaps, then the court will say, "Look, the old king dodders." They will remember he is no true king. They will see you — young, handsome, vigorous, the man to lead them.'

The anger had left his face. He looked almost amused. 'You promised me no honey.'

I looked at him steadily, or as steadily as I could with frozen feet and a nose about to turn to ice. 'Nor do I give you any, my lord.'

He said suddenly, 'You are cold.'

Is that the genius they teach you in Wittenberg, I thought, that a girl in silk in a snowdrift might be cold? 'Yes, my lord.'

I hoped we would go indoors. We could talk by the fire in the great hall.

'Here.' He swept off his cloak and placed it around my shoulders. He was close enough that I could smell his breath: peppermint and musk. His hands felt warm. The cloak was warm from his body too; thick black leather and fur-lined, so long it trailed on the ground. He looked down at my sodden slippers, then scooped me up and placed me on a wooden bench, kicking off the snow in one swift movement.

Instinctively I curled my feet up under the cloak. He grinned and wrapped the cloak around me as if I were a baby. He looked quite different when he grinned.

'Are all the ladies of the court like you?'

'No, my lord,' I said honestly. 'But I try to appear like them.'

'If I had known there was one like you here, I would not have stayed so long at Wittenberg.'

He was flirting. I answered seriously, ignoring his sudden playfulness. 'No, my lord. You shouldn't have stayed away so long. Especially now, with young Fortinbras on the border.'

Even my brother had come home from Paris for the country's crisis. But not Prince Hamlet.

'Fortinbras? What about him?'

'He has an army, and marches at our borders. You did not know?'

'No,' he said slowly. 'My mother's letters never mentioned him.'

'Perhaps Her Majesty did not want to worry you and disturb your studies.'

We exchanged a quick glance.

'Or perhaps,' he said, 'she did not want me to worry and come home.'

He pushed the fur of his cloak closer to my cheek. His hand touched my skin, soft as a butterfly. He looked at me, eyes serious. 'What else should I know about my kingdom?'

'In truth, sir, there is little that should worry you.'

'Beyond an invasion? Or my mother marrying my uncle? Or my kingdom being stolen by my uncle?'

'It is still your kingdom, my lord, if you will stay to take it. And Fortinbras? Even if he invades, each lord has an army to bring to battle, and they will. They may not love your uncle, but neither do they want a stranger ruling over them.'

'I ... see.'

I saw that he did.

'As to the rest,' I continued, 'the land is quiet and well-ordered. The summer harvests were good, and the stockfish was laid in plenty for the winter. The barley granaries are full. The palace has a full twenty-five tons of salted butter, nearly two tons of new cheese and thirty-two of old —'

'Hold.' He looked amused. 'Who is this, with a face like summer's roses and all the wisdom of a chancellor?'

'The lord chancellor's daughter, sir. Who listens. And reads.'

'A woman who reads. A miracle indeed. And who listens too. Then you are Ophelia.'

'I am, my lord.' I smiled at him over the fur of his cloak. 'You last saw me up an apple tree.'

'I have never climbed an apple tree.'

'No, my lord. But I did.'

He laughed. The gloom had vanished. Even the low afternoon sun had rolled out from below a cloud and now tinged the snow with gold. 'I remember you now. Eating apples.'

Actually the apples had been too green to eat; I'd planned to throw them at my nurse when she discovered me. I would have pelted him too, if he hadn't been a prince.

'Yes,' I said. One does not argue with a prince.

His smile faded. He looked at me steadily. 'Well, Ophelia of the wheat-gold hair, will you be my guide to Elsinore? Help me to win the court to my cause?'

'Yes, my lord.' I meant it too. Not because he was the prince who might one day be king, but because I had never spoken to a young man like this. I had never spoken so openly to anyone before, except a ghost, if he had been real, and not a dream.

'An army of two,' he said. He lifted my hand and kissed it, his lips upon my skin. I shivered and saw him smile; Prince Hamlet had kissed women before. 'Will you help me because my cause is just?'

He would be able to tell if I lied. I knew that I didn't do it well.

I said softly, 'Your cause is just, my lord. But I think I would help you even if it weren't.'

'Why? For love of me?'

He spoke lightly, but he meant it too. I loved him then. Not because he was a prince, whose position I had loved long before I saw the man. I loved him for his loneliness. All my life at the court, I had never seen anyone as alone as he was. He seemed as fragile as an icicle that could be burned away by the sun. I loved him because he needed me, not as a decoration for his table, not to keep the linen mended, but for everything I truly was.

I said quietly, 'Yes, my lord. For love of you.' My blush burned my ears.

He knew I didn't lie. I thought he might laugh, but he just nodded. He looked almost as shocked as I.

'I thought to have a kingdom by this day's night,' he said. 'It seems I have a kingdom of the heart, not of the land.'

He bent and kissed me lightly on the lips. He tasted of snow. His kiss lingered long after his lips had gone. When he spoke again, his voice was light, but I could tell he was serious. His gloom had vanished and there was an edge of laughter in his voice.

'Well, wise counsellor, what do I do now?'

'You wait upon your mother, when she goes to her room to change after the feast. I will fetch you,' I added quickly. 'So you may see her before your uncle comes to her.'

'To tell her that I approve of her marriage to my father's brother? Frailty, thy name is woman! By my life, I cannot.'

'No, sir. Nor would your mother believe it. But tell her you will accept it — for her sake, and the country's.'

And because you have no choice, I thought.

He hesitated, half amused at my presumption, but wholly serious as he listened to my words. At last he nodded. 'Very well.'

'Sir, your nose is turning blue.'

He smiled again. 'Can you still love a man with a blue nose?'

'I could love a man with a violet for a nose. But I'd rather that you kept your own.'

He laughed. I felt a thrill run through me, that I had turned his sadness into joy. His moods changed as suddenly as cream turning into butter.

'Inside then,' he said. I scrambled down. It was time we left. Darkness had shrouded his face. The last of the thin winter sun had left the air. He offered me his arm. 'I will walk you to your father's house, Lady Ophelia. You need to change from those damp clothes.' He saw my look, and laughed. 'No more than to your door, I promise.' He lifted my hand again. 'There will be time enough for more. Just say once again that you can love me.'

'Yes, my lord, I tell you truly that I do.'

Nor did I lie. Would I have loved him had he been a woodcutter's son, or even the lord of the exchequer's? I thrust the question from my mind.

Chapter 5

Prince Hamlet left me at our front door, as he'd promised, two servants with flaming torches to light our way. It seemed he did not know about the small door that connected our house and the palace. Or perhaps he wanted the people to see that he escorted me: prince and lord chancellor's daughter together. That is what I would have chosen if I were him. But if I were him, I would not have spent so many years away.

A kingdom needs tending, just like a cheese. Leave a cheese too long and the whey settles to the bottom and sours the whole. Leave a kingdom for too long and others rise to the top and take the whole. I hoped Prince Hamlet was beginning to think like a ruler now, and not the student he had been.

Gerda clucked at me, and changed my stockings and petticoat and slippers. My overdress was damp, but it would do. I slipped along the torchlit passageways and back to the banquet hall. The queen raised her eyebrows as I sat back in my place. I nodded slightly to show her all was well.

The prince's attendants were well into the wine now, slicing cheese and eating pickled herring as well as olives and candied chestnuts sent from France. All the court were eating and laughing. Too determinedly laughing to show their new king that no treason was being plotted.

The banquet ended early; perhaps because neither bride nor groom was young and wished to dance away the night. More likely, they, like all the court, wanted to find out what Prince Hamlet was doing. Sending messages to any lords not here at court to ask for their support? Stripping the treasury of jewels to pay an army? I was sure the man I had met in the garden would do neither. Probably he had been away from court too long for either even to occur to him. But the palace would be a hive of bees tonight, buzzing with gossip.

I waited till Lady Hilda and Lady Anna had removed the queen's headdress, and Lady Annika was dozing as she warmed the queen's shift before the fire, then kneeled before her.

'Madam, there is one who would speak with you.'

Her eyes met mine. She knew this game exactly.

'May I have leave to fetch him, Your Majesty?'

She gave me her hand to kiss. 'You may.'

I heard silence as thick as clotted cream behind me as the maids opened the door. Two of them accompanied me, walking behind except to open the doors that blocked the winter draughts. Earlier, those doors had been left open to let the royal procession pass without waiting. The prince's rooms were one floor up, towards the main tower; the same rooms he'd had since childhood. A footman joined us along the way. One of the mysterious charms of the palace was the way servants appeared just as you needed them, though I knew the magic was in training a good servant in the art of watching. And what not to see while watching.

I paused at the door of the prince's chamber, and let the footman knock and open the door. 'Your Royal Highness,' he intoned, 'the Lady Ophelia.'

'Madam?'

The prince wore black still, but not his travelling clothes. This was black velvet, so dark it seemed to drink the light. He had put on his prince's crown, a plain circle of gold. His face was sombre, but when his eyes met mine, they were warmer than the fire.

I curtseyed deeply. 'I come from your good mother, Your Royal Highness. She may receive you now.'

I knew my words and his would be repeated throughout the servants' hall, and find their way up to their masters' chambers before the hour was past.

'Then I will go to her. I thank you, gentle messenger.'

I let him lead the way, as was proper, the servants and footman trailing behind us. We waited, still in a line, for the footman to open the door to the queen's bedchamber.

'His Royal Highness, the Prince Hamlet,' he announced. 'And the Lady Ophelia.'

The queen rose from the chair by the fire. Her hair was undone, brushed down her back, a little red among the grey. She wore the purple dress still, but had covered it with a black lace shawl. Was this to show her son that she still mourned his father? Yes, I thought. Her role tonight would be as calculated as her son's, and mine.

She held out her hand. 'Hamlet, my dearest son.'

They were words for us to hear, and for the servants. But I heard warmth in her voice too. For this man *was* her son, her only child. Whatever she has kept from him, whatever she has taken from him, I thought, she loves him still.

He kneeled before her, waited for her hand to bid him rise. She offered him her cheek to kiss. He pressed his lips upon it. I felt a tension leave the room; a breeze of breaths exhaled.

'I am glad to see you well, my son. And more glad to see you home than I have power of words to express.'

'I am glad to see you well too, madam.' He turned and met my eyes. 'And to be home.'

More breaths, drawn in now, and whispers not yet spoken. 'Did you see how he looked at Lady Ophelia?' they would mutter later. 'Did you see how she gazed at him? And how the queen smiled upon them both?'

Silence stretched. The queen was waiting for more from Hamlet: congratulations on her marriage; sympathy for her loss. But he said nothing.

A second before the silence began to strain, she asked, 'Will you wait upon your stepfather, the king, tomorrow?'

'Yes, madam, I will greet my stepfather.' Again the pause lengthened before he added, 'The king.'

I let out my own breath. Well-played, I thought. Not quite acceptance, but not rebellion either. The court will remember this. And his mother understood it.

Men's laughter floated down the hall. The king approached. I glanced at Prince Hamlet; he heard it too.

So did the queen.

'Go then, my dear Ophelia, and guide our son back to his chambers, in case he forgets the ways of Elsinore.'

It was a warning, and a gift.

Prince Hamlet accepted both. He stepped back and took my hand, and raised it to his lips for all to see. 'Some flowers bloom despite the winter chill.'

He bowed — a son's bow, not a courtier's — to his mother, then offered me his arm.

I glanced at the queen. She nodded. So I took the prince's arm and walked with him along the silent corridor as the bawdy jokes of the king's men filled the corridors below.

The queen's footman was at our house the next morning with a message for me to wait upon Her Majesty. I had expected it and risen early, my candle nibbling at the dark. The morning after a royal bedding was as public as the wedding.

I'd had Gerda dress me in cream silk, with swansdown at the cuffs and hem; not mourning, but not coloured either. The footman held the torch as I slipped through the door that linked us to the palace. It was too cold and dark to use the front entrance so early in the day.

The queen was still abed, alone. Whatever had happened in the night, the king was gone now. Lady Annika sat before the fire, warming her hands and the queen's shift. Lady Anna and Lady Hilda added attar of roses to the washing water. All three wore black silk with satin overskirts. I blushed to think I had mistaken the morning's mood.

But the queen smiled at me. 'A summer's bloom indeed, my young white rose.' She held out her hand for me to kiss.

We washed and dressed her: in black this morning too, a widow, not a bride, with purple stones at her ears and a small ruff also of purple.

Lady Hilda called for breakfast. We sat and embroidered as the queen ate her barley bread, fresh baked that morning and dipped in ale we heated with a poker from the fire; hot barley porridge with salted butter and a compote of dried fruits in damson wine; cold meats from the night before, well-minced to suit the queen's age and lack of teeth; and Queen's Cream cheese, named in her honour and so soft there was no need to chew.

I had hoped Prince Hamlet might join her for breakfast. He didn't. Perhaps he was tired from his journey, of both body and emotions, the day before. Probably he thought his uncle might be here too. I wondered if I would have a chance to see him before he presented himself to the king this morning. A queen may call a man to her. A lady-in-waiting waits: for the queen to finish eating before she eats too; for a prince to call her, or for his mother to send her to him. I waited.

At last the queen finished, and we four ate. There was some Queen's Cream left. I waited again, in case the more senior ladies wanted it, then swallowed it all with chunks of bread, suddenly ravenous.

It was mid-morning by the time the queen was ready to go to the throne room. We proceeded down the corridors, three black ducklings and a white one, behind the wider, richer skirts of our queen. The torches flickered, holding back the gloom. The horizon was still grey as the midwinter sun struggled to rise out of the stones of winter's night.

The chamber doors opened. I bit back a gasp. Yesterday there had been one throne up on the dais, gold, or gilded, with rubies inset across the head. Beside it had sat a chair with red silk cushions, where the queen had sat beside her lord. Today, two thrones stood there side by side.

A lady-in-waiting knows what not to see. I kept all expression from my face as the queen glided down the room and sat upon her throne. She let her hands rest upon the arms, as if she and her throne had grown together. As, I thought, they had.

I remembered when I was a child, the royal beekeeper had shown me the hives. He'd meant it as a lesson: don't go too near when the bees are among the apple trees or you'll be stung. But I was fascinated.

'Only one queen in every hive,' he'd said. 'All the young bees are her children. And when she dies, they raise a new queen to take her place.'

'What about the king?' I'd asked.

He'd laughed. 'No kings in beehives, missy. Only the queen.'

If there had been no wedding yesterday, I thought, there would be no second throne. Now Denmark had a king and queen as equals. A true queen, a ruler in her hive.

'Lady Ophelia.' I blinked as Lady Annika nudged me. 'The queen has given us leave to go.'

To go? But the queen was always attended by her ladies. Soon Prince Hamlet would come here to the throne room, and the king would tell him formally that he was both son and heir.

And then I understood. The queen might rule with the king now, but this was still a parliament of men. The queen would be the only woman in this room while state business was discussed.

I followed the others out, as the youngest, then stood aside to allow the king and his retinue to enter. We curtseyed deeply. I looked up through my lashes, but there was no sign of Prince Hamlet. Of course not, I thought. He would not join the king's retinue.

We straightened, then sank into a curtsey again. For here was the prince. Black silk stockings, black leather boots trimmed with bear fur. The boots stopped in front of me. A white hand wearing a gold ring with a black stone extended from his fur-lined sleeve. 'My Lady Ophelia.'

I took his hand as I rose from my curtsey, and felt mine kissed; another true kiss, lips on skin.

'Good morning to the rose of Elsinore.' His voice was light, a courtier's words, but I could hear the warmth below.

'Good morning, Your Royal Highness.'

He smiled, made a short bow, then he was gone, into the throne room. The footmen closed the chamber doors behind him.

Lady Anna cackled. 'So that is how the wind blows, eh?'

'So like his father,' murmured Lady Annika vaguely.

'No,' said Lady Hilda quickly. 'He favours his mother surely.'

Lady Annika seemed to wake up at that. 'Ah, yes. I had forgot. The prince has his mother's eyes.'

'And someone else's heart,' said Lady Anna.

I blushed, my cheeks as hot as the hall fire.

Chapter 6

It seemed I had a morning of freedom if the queen was going to be in council. Lady Annika, Lady Anna and Lady Hilda tottered down to the great hall, and the castle's largest fire, to sit with their embroideries. I didn't join them. I pitied anyone who had to sit on the lumps my tapestry made of chairs.

What to do? I could go home: inspect the furs in the garderobe for moth; order new sweet rushes for the floors to get rid of some of the fug of winter; make more bilberry and willow cordial for Lady Hilda to ease her indigestion. But I wanted to know what was being said behind the closed doors of the throne room. It might take a day for palace gossip to reach our kitchen, and then filter upstairs to Gerda and to me. Here, in the hum of the palace, a servant serving hot wine and ale would hear what Prince Hamlet said to the new King Claudius, what the queen said, and how they all looked. By midday I might know it too.

And if I stayed in the palace, I'd have a chance to see

Prince Hamlet. He might stay with the king and queen and council now — I hoped he did, to begin to understand the ruling of his country — but he would not dine with his uncle. Back to his rooms? No. Too like a sulky child.

I grinned. I knew exactly where he would go.

The library was a long room, with fires at each end that were lit throughout winter to keep the books and manuscripts and maps dry and free of mould, and torches along the walls. Winter's thin light was too small for the large room. I doubted the late king had ever been in the room, but some earlier king had stocked it well.

There were books written in the ornamental scripts of monks, bright with reds and scatterings of gold; large manuscripts rolled up and carefully stored; printed books of quarto paper with leather covers finely stitched. Most were in Greek or Latin, which, as a girl, I had not been taught to read. But some had been translated by a long-gone monk — I recognised the same hand in them all. How many years had he sat here, I wondered, twisting words from one tongue to another? What king had ordered him to do so, and why? Or had it been a queen — a girl like me perhaps, untutored in Greek and Latin but curious to read about the world?

I took out my favourite book. Indeed, it was so well-loved I had left fingermarks along its edge, though I doubted anyone would notice for generations to come. It was called *Great Dialogues of Plato*, but was about another man called Socrates. A man who questioned rather than ruled, who talked of good and evil. Had he been a king? The book didn't say. I didn't think he was. He talked about his friends, not his subjects.

I would have asked my father or my brother who Socrates had been, but then they would have realised I came here, and might have forbidden it. It is well-known that too much learning sends a woman mad. But I was not mad yet, and I had found I could best be a good daughter by making sure my father never guessed what to forbid. Why couldn't my father be like Socrates? My father proclaimed; he did not discuss. And yet, I thought, Socrates had a daughter and a wife, but there were no women included in his and his friends' dinner conversations.

I took my book as close as I dared to the fire without scorching my skirts. If I had been in my own rooms, I would have lifted my skirts to warm my legs, but a footman might come in at any moment to bid me to attend the queen. I had told no one where I was going, but the servants always knew.

I opened the book and started reading my favourite conversation: about the kinds of love. So many kinds, and yet they did not talk of the love of a mother for her child, or a queen for her people. Socrates's friends needed a woman there, I thought, to teach them of the world beyond the experience of men. Plato didn't even mention what they ate for dinner as they talked. What people eat tells you a lot about them. The old king had liked bear steaks, red and bloody, or boar he'd speared himself. King Claudius dined on venison with French sauces. My father liked plain roast mutton, well-cooked, or stuffed pike. My cheeses talked to me not just of the seasons, but of the kingdom beyond the palace: spring grass up in the summer-grazing meadows, or autumn blight upon the farmer's hay …

A soft laugh interrupted me. 'The stars have come to dance with us, and arrows play upon the air. A girl who reads!'

'Your Highness.' I turned around and curtseyed quickly as Prince Hamlet strode down the room towards me.

'This is the one place in the palace where we can be sure of being alone,' he said. 'I doubt anyone except you has come here since I left for Wittenberg.'

Apart from the servants, I thought. How does the prince think the books are kept free of dust, their covers oiled, the fire lit? But I had never known a man to think of such things.

'Sir, how did you find …' I was going to say 'the king' but changed it to, 'the court this morning?'

He shrugged, his brightness turning back to shadow as fast as cloud passes the sun. 'Well, well, well.'

'You are named heir?'

'I am. And I will not return to Wittenberg.'

I sat down without thinking, I was so relieved. 'I am so glad. Oh, my lord, I beg your pardon!' I stood again.

He chuckled, his gloom gone as quickly as it had come, and kissed me lightly on the cheek. 'There, I have been thinking of doing that ever since I saw you. Sit, my dear Ophelia. Should a daisy bow its head, or a rose stare at the ground? Sit or stand as you will, forever in my presence.'

'I thank you, sir.' I sat down again and hugged my knees, suddenly as easy as if he'd been my brother. 'What else was said in council?'

He looked at me, amused. 'Yesterday I thought that frailty's name was woman. Now I find a girl of steel who would rather talk of council matters than of love.'

'I … I … Sir, I will talk of love if that is what you wish. But you said you needed a guide here at the court.'

'And I have found one. My friend Horatio arrived from Wittenberg last week. He left after me, but had a faster voyage by ship. He chose to be on watch last night,' his face clouded for an instant, 'instead of attending the feast.'

'I … I am glad you have another friend here now, my lord.'

I thought of the two thrones side by side. I must show this prince that a girl could be as valuable a counsel as his friend Horatio.

He sat on the sofa and took my hand and pressed it to his lips. 'An hour ago the world was weary, stale, unprofitable, heavy on my shoulders as an avalanche of snow. And now here I find you, and the sunbeams gleam like spring.'

All at once I realised I had no maid here, nor footman, no chaperone at all. But surely the usual rules did not apply to princes. The queen herself had bid me to walk and talk with him. And Prince Hamlet had kissed me in front of the ladies of the court. One day this man would be our king, and kings and queens made the rules ... and could break them.

Prince Hamlet still held my hand. Suddenly he frowned. 'Perhaps you may guide me yet, my lily, my rosemary branch. Horatio told me something that troubles me.'

Something more than his uncle stealing his mother and his throne?

'What, my lord?'

'Have you heard talk ... gossip ... about a ghost who haunts the palace?'

'Yes, my lord.'

He let my hand fall. Whatever he had been expecting, it wasn't that. 'You have heard talk? Or you have seen the ghost yourself?'

His face was so dark I was alarmed.

'I ... I thought I saw a ghost, years ago. But it was a child's dream, no more. Night after night I went back up to the battlements, but it was never there again.'

'You were a child?' he asked sharply.

'Yes, my lord. Six years old.'

He sat back, his eyes clouded. 'This ghost is born new, hanging helpless between heaven and earth. You have not met any other?'

'My lord, I am sure I would have remembered if I had. It was a dream.'

'A dream. Yes.' He sat quietly, as if thinking. 'Last night Horatio was on watch with two guardsmen, Marcellus and Bernardo. Do you know them?'

'I have heard their names, my lord.'

'They seem good men. And Horatio is a scholar and a friend. And yet, they told me that last midnight as the clock chimed they saw ...' His voice faded, as if he could not say the words.

'A ghost, my lord?'

'Yes,' he whispered. The joy had gone from his face again.

'My lord,' I said cautiously, 'the wine flowed freely last night, and brandy too. I warrant even the watch drank their fill. At midnight in midwinter, a man might see a wisp of mist, a snowfall, or even a petticoat blowing in the wind, and think it a ghost.'

'They say they saw my father's ghost,' he said flatly.

I tried to choose my words carefully. 'Last night, of all nights, loyal men might well have seen your father's face in the snowflakes about the palace. Any man who did not say "Nay" when the priest asked for objections to the marriage had reason to imagine King Hamlet's face at midnight.'

He sat silent again, then took my hand and held it tight, as much for comfort, it seemed to me, as for love.

'I think that you are right,' he said.

'I think that you are gloomy again, my lord. Can we not talk of brighter news?'

He gave me a wry smile. 'Of Fortinbras, now sent to Poland by his angry uncle, no longer a wolf to snap at Denmark's heels? He asks permission for his troops to pass through Denmark, but as a friend, not conqueror.'

So the queen was right. As soon as Fortinbras knew he would have to face a strong king and true opposition, any plans to invade had vanished. But I could not say all that to Hamlet.

I clapped my hands in delight. 'Truly, that is wondrous news!'

He smiled properly then. 'Oh, brave new world that has such girls in it. If I gave you flowers, would you rather they were council papers?'

'If you gave me flowers, I … I would treasure them, as I would any gift of yours.'

'And if I gave you a ring?' he asked lightly.

My heart thudded so loudly I was sure that he could hear it. 'I would treasure that too, my lord, my whole life, if it came from you.'

Someone coughed discreetly. The door had opened and I hadn't even heard it. My father and brother might not know I came here to the library, but every servant did.

'Her Majesty calls for you, my lady,' said the footman, his face carefully blank.

'I come at once,' I said. 'My lord, if I have your leave?'

'Only if you leave to come again.'

'I will.'

My heart sang as I lifted my skirts and hurried along the shadowed corridor, as if the birds had decided it was already spring.

Chapter 7

It was warm in my bed cabinet with its doors shut against the draughts. I lay under the quilt and waited for the darkness to seep into my brain. Instead, it just felt stuffy. How could I sleep? All I had dreamed had come true.

Today, Prince Hamlet had spoken of offering me a ring. He had chosen me himself, not had me put forward as a useful match by his mother, to keep the support of my father and his estates. And I loved him. Surely I loved him? His kisses made me shiver. He fascinated me, this stranger come from Wittenberg, so unlike the courtiers I saw day after day, more in love with hunting and quaffing than with their wives. Poor lonely prince. He needed me.

He had been so troubled this morning, thinking that his father's ghost might walk the earth on the night of his wife's wedding to his brother.

Were ghosts real? I was no child now, to believe in them. Even when I had crept up to the tower again, I had not really believed I would find King Fortinbras there.

'Nonsense,' Nurse had said when I'd told her the old king walked at night. She'd looked at me suspiciously. 'Have you been eating cheese at bedtime again, my girl?'

Outside, the wind muttered, rattling the shutters, as though it strove to come in. As the ghosts of men might strive to make the living remember why they must haunt the battlements: one robbed of his kingdom; the other of his wife and his son's inheritance. It was easy to imagine ghosts in midwinter, when the darkness leached all light except the stars.

What if there truly had been a ghost up on the battlements all those years ago? What if my meeting with King Fortinbras's ghost was real? If that ghost was real, perhaps King Hamlet's was too, and would continue to walk the battlements until his son and heir was king.

And yet …

King Hamlet had cared little for his son while he was alive. So little that he had never called him home from Wittenberg. Would he really walk in the wind and dark of the night, seeking justice for his son?

I did not think so.

There would be no ghosts up on the battlements; but there would be fresh air. I'd had enough of winter fires and fug and palace walls. I pushed open the bed-cabinet doors and slid down onto the cold rushes laid on the floor. Long ago I had learned that there was only one time a girl could be truly free: night, when all in the castle but its guards and porters were asleep. A time when rats danced, and owls swooped on careless mice, and the stars waltzed across the heavens, when a girl could feel the whispers of the darkness with no one calling her to unlock the store cupboard or help a queen undress.

I reached under my mattress and found my freedom clothes — breeches, doublet and hose, a man's leather shoes, a short half-cloak. Laertes had outgrown them at fourteen. They fitted me perfectly. They were brown and made me part of the castle's shadows. And if someone did glimpse me, who can tell one face from another in the flicker of torchlight?

I slipped along the corridor. The door to the palace opened smoothly; I made sure the servants kept it well-oiled. Down the main corridor, then along a small one, dusty, for the maids cleaned here only in spring. There was the door to the servants' privy, and next to it another door, which might be to a cupboard.

I took out the key from my shoe. I'd taken it years ago, first to lock the door behind me when I was up in the tower, so no one could find me, and then to keep the door locked even when I wasn't there. A locked tower can be overlooked if it is small and narrow and too badly sited to use to shoot arrows or pour hot butter down upon your enemies. I suspected it had been built as access for the builders to build the privy chimney, and forgotten for hundreds of years. Except by me.

I locked the door behind me, then climbed the narrow stairs. Round once, twice, and I was pushing open the dwarf-sized door. I found fresh air — too much of it.

The wind punched and battered me, and set my cloak flapping. I pulled it close, then sat on my favourite stone on the ledge, feeling the fresh air upon my face.

I could smell the sea, the forest, the cold stones of the graveyard below, the lingering smoke from the braziers the servants had placed in the royal garden to warm the queen when she had taken a brief stroll in the sun. I could smell the world from here!

If only I could fly with the wind — to Wittenberg or across the waves to Norway or England. Or even deal with such places through letters and messengers, like my father did. Let my mind travel, while my body stayed here. For truly, I loved Denmark too much to want to leave. I could not believe that English cows were fatter than ours, or French cheeses creamier.

Did they even make cheese in a university town like Wittenberg? I could be queen of infinite space if only I was allowed to let my mind free, instead of being crabbed and confined by embroidery and curtseying. I seemed to have spent half my life in a curtsey.

Above me the moon sailed like a vast gold ducat across the sky, throwing shadows almost as distinct as those of the winter sun. On the high battlements beyond, I saw figures move. The men of the watch, though there was no enemy army to watch for tonight.

If Fortinbras tried to climb these walls, our men could pour boiling butter down on them. And we women would huddle inside, until the men had decided the day. Yet it was our hands that made the butter, and the cheeses and dried barley loaves, so we might eat in a castle under siege by army or by winter.

What was Hamlet doing tonight? Sleeping, I hoped, with no nightmare dreams about his father's ghost.

The wind moaned and muttered, almost as if its song had words. The mist clung to the castle walls ... Not mist. A ghost. Hovering just above the battlements. I should be scared, I thought. But it was as though I was meeting an old friend.

'You look the same,' I whispered.

King Fortinbras smiled. A sad smile, his kind eyes filled with empty shadows. 'The dead do not age. Ten years is the tinny twinkle of a star.'

'But I'm older.'

'Older, but just the same. The girl was the seed of the woman. I have watched you grow, child, night by night upon this tower.'

'I'm not a child.' I lifted my chin. 'I will be queen. You said I'd make a good queen.'

He nodded. I could see the moonlight behind his face. 'I did. Whose queen will you be?'

'My own. And my people's.'

He smiled again. 'A good answer. I should have asked, how will you become this queen?'

'The prince of Denmark loves me. Prince Hamlet.'

The smile faded. 'That is not a name I can love. It was Hamlet who stole my kingdom. Now Hamlet, son of Hamlet, will steal you as his bride.'

'No theft, Sir Ghost. I give myself willingly. More than willingly.'

The wind screamed, battering the walls. The ghost was silent. I thought: this man was a warrior. Now he is the ghost of one. And I have said that I am to marry the son of his once mortal enemy.

But what could a ghost do to me? If a ghost could lift a sword, he would be avenged already.

'Your Majesty ... you told me long ago that ghosts must linger between earth and heaven till the injustice done to them has been avenged.' I took a deep breath. 'Do you seek revenge on Prince Hamlet now?'

'The wind and I shall keep company above this castle till I am avenged. Vengeance will happen. It is almost done. Yet I do not seek it.'

'I don't understand.'

Those sad shadow eyes gazed at me. 'Kindness returns to the giver. So does hatred. I left my son no kingdom, no castle, but I can give him this. I will not ask him to avenge me, to breed more hate. Hate begets hate, generation unto generation. Kindness breeds joys. Remember this, my child. Give with love, and love will repay you sevenfold.'

'I ... I will.'

'Other ghosts might haunt their sons and cry, "Avenge me." But not King Fortinbras.' The mist faded, but his smile seemed like the moonlight, lingering on. 'Remember, sweet Ophelia. Remember me ...'

'I will remember,' I whispered.

I sat there in my borrowed cloak. Would he appear again? He had said he'd watched me over the years. Was he watching still, part of the night?

What power had a ghost? Power to influence the thoughts of men. And girls. King Fortinbras could have tried to turn me against Hamlet, son and namesake of his enemy. Instead, he had told me to give, with love.

He had also said that his vengeance had almost come. He must mean that with the death of old King Hamlet he would soon be free.

'Sleep well, Sir Ghost,' I said softly to the darkness.

His blessing seemed as warm as another cloak about my shoulders. A life of love, here in the palace. Love spilling across the kingdom. Every cheese-maker knows that cheese tastes best when made with love. A kingdom ruled with love must be better too.

I hugged my knees, and smelled the wind, and dreamed of love, and Prince Hamlet.

Chapter 8

The snow outside sang to me as Gerda stirred up the bedroom fire the next morning. I had slept late, too filled with happiness to fall asleep easily after my expedition to the tower. Now the sun shone her first beams across the snow, turning the world from black to white. I could have danced across the room like a snowflake. But a lady waits to be dressed properly. And this morning, I was a lady again.

'What dress today, my lady?' asked Gerda.

She had been my mother's maid, and then mine since I grew too old to have a nurse.

'The green with silver lacing.'

The queen had forbidden the court to wear black for King Hamlet now that she and King Claudius were wed, yet too bright a dress might offend his son. But I was tired of lavenders and white.

Gerda built up the fire. It blazed away the cold. Even my feet were warm on the bearskin by my bed as Gerda put up the screens and washed me with rosewater, then slid on a fresh shift, a petticoat of silver, the green overskirt and green sleeves.

A footman brought in my breakfast: warm ale with rye bread sopped in it, and cold venison — the king must have found time to hunt in the past few days, I thought, as well as to marry — and half a dozen Hardy Orange cheeses, each one no bigger than a walnut. They were laid in straw baskets on our estates in summer, till the whey dripped out and a grassy mould grew a skin to protect the cheese inside. You had to cellar a Hardy Orange carefully — a break in the skin would send it bad.

I cut into the first one. Perfect, as it should be. A good household and a good estate meant excellent cheese.

'Has my father breakfasted?'

'Hours ago, my lady, with Lord Laertes,' said Gerda. 'They have gone to the council chamber.'

I nodded. While Laertes had been in Paris, Father had talked to me of state business over breakfast, for lack of any other audience for his speeches: how many ships of stockfish were needed to feed the people through winter, when the ships could no longer sail, and through the hungry spring until the harvest; if the rye crop had gone well, or had been attacked by rust; how the French king had married his daughter to the king of Scotland to seal an alliance. My father had his son home again to share his talk now, but Laertes was to start back to Paris this afternoon. Perhaps tomorrow my father might share the world with me again.

I motioned Gerda to sit on the small stool by my side. When we were alone, I had her eat with me. She took a tankard of the ale and dunked her bread in it.

I spread a thick slice of Hardy Orange over my bread, and took a bite. 'What is the talk in the servants' hall?'

Gerda lowered her voice, even though there was no one else to hear. 'Oh, such a fuss, my lady. Lady Annika's maid is big with child. We've known for weeks, though she tried to hide it with tight lacing. But now the man will marry her, so all is well.'

'Who is he?'

'The palace blacksmith's son, apprenticed to the trade.'

'Didn't his sister …' I stopped.

'Oh, yes, that was sad. The one who drowned herself in the stream for love.'

Or for despair, I thought. If a maid gave herself to her lover and he did not marry her, what could the girl do — her honour gone, no way to feed herself and her child? Few families, poor or rich, would keep a daughter after she had disgraced their house. The palace blacksmith had shut the door upon his daughter, and now she lay, her unborn child with her, in a suicide's grave outside the churchyard. Even death had not washed her sins away.

'Other news,' I pleaded. 'Happier news.'

Gerda's smile returned. 'Oh, there's very happy news, my lady. News of love, and a wedding in the summer. The whole palace is talking about it.'

'Whose wedding?'

'Why, yours, my lady.'

I flushed and looked down at my bread and cheese. Was there a servant hidden behind every tapestry that lined the palace walls? 'There has been no talk of weddings.'

'But there has been of love?'

I didn't answer.

The doors opened. A footman in the queen's red and gold brocade bowed low. 'Her Majesty would see you, my lady.'

I stood quickly; you did not keep a queen waiting, even if you were in the privy. I was glad the summons hadn't come before I was properly dressed. 'Where is Her Majesty?'

'In the solar, my lady.'

The footman followed me along the corridors to open the doors for me, and Gerda followed too, carrying my silver fox cloak lined with green velvet in case the queen wished me to accompany her into the royal garden. Today's sun might tempt her into the fresh air. The palace draughts snickered about my skirts and I almost asked for the cloak now. But that would be unseemly, as if accusing the king and queen of such poor hospitality that their company must wear their cloaks indoors.

The solar faced south, with thick glass in its windows and braziers around the room, as well as the big fire, to keep it as warm as summer. The queen sat on a silk cushion, her ladies on cushions too, sewing their tapestries. Or rather Lady Hilda and Lady Anna sewed, and Lady Annika dozed. In the past year she had managed to stitch only the nose of the hound in her tapestry. I doubted the poor beast would ever be granted an ear, much less a tail.

I curtseyed deeply. 'Your Majesty. I hope I see you well.'

The queen smiled. 'You do.'

She did look well — a new husband in her bed, a new throne, her son home in her palace. And the old king, my mind whispered, with his cruel jokes and mistresses, safely gone.

'I have a task for you, my dear.'

'Of course, Your Majesty. Your will is mine.'

She laughed. 'I am glad to hear it. Would you carry an ox for me to Paris?'

'Of course, Your Majesty.'

'And sweep a mountain free of snow so I could climb it?'

I smiled too. 'Whatever Your Majesty wishes.'

'Then this is today's task. You will walk with my son, and make him smile. His temper has too much of winter in it. Can you manage that, do you think?'

I curtseyed again, hoping it hid my flush. I heard a maid giggle. 'I hope I can fulfil Your Majesty's will.'

'Then off with you. Enjoy the brief sunlight while you may. Leave us old crones to our sewing, and be young.'

'Your Majesty will never be old,' I said. 'You are like the sun, newborn each day.'

'An excellent answer.'

I heard laughter behind me as I left.

* * *

He was waiting for me in the great hall. Gerda had
been summoned to bring fur-lined boots, a fur hat,
fur gloves and muff, and a green silk jacket lined with
felted lambswool to go beneath my coat. Lucky lamb, I
thought, to wear only one pelt, when a lady must wear
twenty. But at least I would be warm.

I stepped up to the prince and curtseyed as gracefully
as I could in six layers of silk and linen and fur. 'My lord,
your gracious mother bids me to walk with you.'

He took my hand to raise me from the curtsey. 'I am
glad.'

He didn't look glad. He looked tired. More than that,
I thought, suddenly worried: he looked as if the life
was being drained from him with each hour he spent at
Elsinore. The queen was right. He must be made to smile.

Gerda began to follow us down the palace steps.

Hamlet waved her back. 'Your mistress has no need of
you now.'

'But, Your Highness ...' Gerda halted, looking at me
helplessly. A maid must obey a prince.

I glanced back at her, uncertain. A young girl shouldn't
walk alone with a man. But this was the prince, and I
had the queen's permission. Not just that. Her order. And
I wanted to walk! To dance! Away from the smoke and
shadows of the palace, the intrigues of the past month. I
wanted to feel the snow break like a bread crust under my
feet; breathe deep of air with all the shadows frozen out.

And, whispered a small voice inside me, Prince Hamlet cannot kiss you with Gerda looking.

Would he ask me to marry him today? Was that why he wished to walk with me alone?

We walked across the palace courtyard, over the drawbridge and into the marketplace. The people stood back to let us pass, bowing and curtseying. Despite my arm resting on his, Hamlet seemed far away. Was his mind back at Wittenberg?

I stayed silent as we crossed the marketplace, then walked down the road. A man bringing firewood for the palace quickly moved his ox and cart out of our way. A woman ran forward to sweep the ox dung away before we dirtied our shoes. I smiled a thank you, though I knew she would value the dung. A high dunghill meant a happy house. The dung fed the fields; the fields fed the cows; the cows fed the cheese; the cheese fed us … I smiled at myself, thinking of dung when I should be thinking of love.

'You look happy, my lady.' The prince looked at me, his eyes like a puppy's that had been beaten.

'I am happy.'

'Why? What is there in this heavy world to smile about?'

I let go of his hand and danced upon the snow, feeling it crunch and squeak under my feet, just as I had imagined. 'Because I am with you. Because the world is washed white and clean with snow. Can't you hear it sing?'

He frowned. 'I hear no birds, no music.'

'The snow sings, my lord. Listen!'

I stood still so he could hear it too; not just the faint crackle and drip as the snow melted in the sun, but the deeper music of the expanse of white.

All at once his frown lightened. 'I think I hear it. You give even winter a sweet voice, my lady.' His eyes were less sombre now. He gestured towards the trees in the king's forest to our right, each branch hung with snow. 'Will you walk in the forest with me?'

I hesitated again. A walk in the woods was different from a walk down the road, with farms on either side. Prince Hamlet must know that the entire palace — even the whole town — would soon know that we had walked alone together. Surely there was only one reason he would so publicly take me walking in the forest. He must be going to ask me to marry him.

I smiled. A girl has a right to privacy when a young man is asking for her hand.

The sun was as high as it would rise today, hovering like a tired orange above the horizon. Hamlet held out his hand. I took it. Our shadows skittered winter black upon the snow. It stuck to my boots, so I had to keep shaking them clean.

Each tree stood like a silent soldier in its armour of white. If there was a path, the snow had hidden it. We ducked under trees. Snow fell off their branches and exploded up in a white powder that stung my face and eyes. All the while Hamlet didn't speak, pushing his way through the branches with a strange eagerness.

I wiped the snow from my cheeks. 'Where are we going, my lord?'

He glanced at me almost as if he had forgotten I was there. 'A place.'

I laughed. I felt as if the pigeons might sing in chorus above us, as if the voles and hedgehogs might wake up and dance about our feet. I was in love with the world today, not just with Hamlet. Poor Hamlet, who had lost so much. But I would make him smile. 'Is there anywhere that is no place?'

He looked at me and seemed as weary as if it was he who carried the great load of snow, not the trees.

'My dreams,' he said abruptly. 'My fears. They are no place. But they are real.' He held out his black-gloved hand to catch a drop of snow melting from a branch. 'At times I wish I could dissolve into dew, like this poor scrap of ice. How weary, stale and unprofitable seem all the uses of this world.' He gestured at the trees around us. 'Life seems an unweeded garden, like this forest, rank, unpruned.'

'Look again, my lord,' I said softly. 'God weeds the forest. It has no need of man, except to give us wood, and beauty.'

He looked at me, not at the trees. But he almost smiled.

'So what is this "place" you take me to, my lord?'

'Can you guess?'

'A flour mill?' With servants to greet us with mulled wine and toasted cheese, I hoped.

He shook his head.

'A woodsman's cottage?' And a woodsman's wife, a fire-cheered kitchen and ham bone soup.

He did smile at that. 'No. It is a place I have not seen for more than ten years, since I left Elsinore. But it is beautiful. As beautiful as you.'

I hoped my smile might bring an echo on his face. 'Perhaps in ten years it has changed.'

His face clouded. I wished I could swallow my words. 'Change? Ay, time eats constancy. Women are the frailest of all.'

One did not argue with a prince. Not even one who said he loved you. I bit my lip to stop my tongue.

'But this place does not change.' He lifted a branch, heavy with snow, which cascaded to the ground with a soft thud. His face relaxed properly for the first time today. 'See, here is my place that lives on earth, and also in my dreams. No rank trees, to sully its purity. What does not grow can never change or putrefy.'

I looked. It was a glade, no larger than my room. A silver snake through the snow showed where a stream would run in summer.

Hamlet gazed around, the depression sliding from him, like snow from the trees. 'When I was locked in my chamber for giggling when the Spanish ambassador tripped in the throne room, when my tutor beat me at school, I thought of this place. Pure, and full of happiness. I came here as a child to fish,' he added softly.

'With your father?'

'My father? No, of course not.' He smiled down at me.

'A king has more important tasks than fishing with his son.'

Like hunting deer and boar, I thought, and bedding mistresses. How well did Hamlet know this father that he mourned? I was beginning to suspect his memory had made the father he would rather have had.

'The jester brought me here. Old Yorick.'

I dimly remembered Yorick: a small man with one shoulder higher than the other and a smile of patient pain. The late king had made him dance with a bear. The bear had lashed out and suddenly Yorick's face was red with blood. The king had laughed, and my father had hurried me from the room. I forced myself back to the king's son, standing with me now.

'Old Yorick told me jokes too.' For the first time, Hamlet's eyes danced at me. 'When can't a fish swim?'

'I don't know, my lord.'

'When it's a dish of fish.' He gave a rueful shrug. 'It seemed funnier when Yorick said it. I caught a fish too. Or rather, Yorick held both lines and when one hooked a fish, he told me it was my line that had caught it. He pretended to be my horse on the way back, and I rode on his shoulders, carrying my fish. He took it to the kitchens, and brought it up to me for my supper, before he attended the king.'

It seemed that Yorick had been more of a father to Hamlet than the king. I wondered if old King Hamlet had even known his son had caught a fish? How could such a man have a son like this? No wonder both father and son had been content for Hamlet to continue his studies rather than helping to run the kingdom. They employed my father to do that.

Hamlet gazed at me. 'Your thoughts are far away, my lady.'

I smiled at him. 'No, of course not. I am here, and my thoughts too.'

'I am a bad companion. Things are ... not as they seemed yesterday.'

I looked at him, alarmed. 'How, my lord?'

Had King Claudius withdrawn his offer to make Hamlet his heir? I could think of nothing else that could weigh him down so much, lower even than when he had realised he had lost not just his father but his kingship.

He hesitated. 'There are more things in heaven and earth than are dreamed of in your philosophy books, Ophelia. Matters too weighty for a girl.'

'I am not a girl! I am your friend. You called me wise counsel.'

His face lightened, as if a ray of sun had caught it. 'You are most certainly a girl, and I a man. Nor would I have you bear what I was shown last night. I have a present for you.'

'Yes, my lord.'

His grimness lessened even more. 'I like it when you say "Yes, my lord" like that. You are a gentle woman. A flower blooming in the dung heap that is Elsinore.'

'No dung heap, my lord. Just cautious lords, who do their best ...'

I stopped as he put his hand into the pouch at his belt. A betrothal ring, I thought. Something glittered in the winter sun. He held it out.

I took it. A gold chain, and on it a heart-shaped locket. Despite my disappointment, its beauty made me catch my breath. It was old gold, almost red, with a polish that came through age and love. I looked at Prince Hamlet in wonder, then opened it. Inside was a lock of hair.

'My lord, thank you! Whose is it?'

A smile almost made its way past the grimness. 'It is yours now. But the locket was my grandmother's. And the hair is mine.' He looked at me so intently, I felt the snow would melt all around us. 'Now you have my heart, Ophelia. I would have you wear it next to your heart too.'

'I will, my lord,' I whispered. I would have danced again if his mood had not been so changeable and grim. Hamlet loved me! What was a ring compared to a prince's heart?

'Let me fasten it for you,' he said.

I felt his gloved hands move clumsily around my neck, and then the locket cold on my skin.

'There,' he said. 'My heart is yours.'

'And you have mine, my lord.'

Why did he not smile again? For we had each other now; our lives and the kingdom stretched in front of us. Or did it? What shadow kept darkening his eyes?

'My lord, what has burdened you so since yesterday?'

'Last night ...' he said, and stopped. He looked so serious. I wanted him to share my joy.

'You saw a ghost last night?' I teased.

He stepped back, his face so white that I was frightened. 'How did you know?'

'I ... I didn't.' I took his hand, as I would take a little boy's. 'My lord, I have met the ghost. He is old King Fortinbras, clinging as mist to the stones of his lost castle. He did me no harm —'

'Old Fortinbras?' He shook his head. 'This was my father's ghost.'

I blinked at him. How many ghosts had appeared last night on the battlements of Elsinore? The castle had many towers, each hidden from the others by the palace roof. I had a sudden picture in my mind of a crowd of ghosts, each arguing who had the right to haunt which tower.

'A ghost cannot hurt you,' I ventured softly.

'Cannot hurt me! My poor father, doomed to wander upon the earth, and you say this cannot hurt me!'

I looked at his face, the anguish written more clearly upon it than the monk's script in the books in the library. I had not liked the old king when he was alive. I liked him even less now. 'I am sorry, my lord. Of course it wounds you.'

'You believe me?'

'Yes, my lord.' I wondered if I should tell him that I had talked to a ghost myself last night. But Prince Hamlet might not approve of my talking to his father's enemy, even though he was dead. 'Your father must be vexed for you, my lord, to see his son's inheritance so delayed.'

Hamlet gazed back in the direction of the palace, almost as if he might see his father's ghost hovering against the whiteness of the snow.

'For me? No, my father's ghost did not speak of me, except to lay me with the duty of a son.' Hamlet looked at me again, his eyes as bleak as a lump of coal. 'My father told me he was murdered.'

Chapter 9

There was a river on our estate, which ran smooth and gentle till it passed a giant rock. And then it fell, swift and unexpected; no more a river but an abyss of mist. I felt I had fallen down that abyss now.

Hamlet had faced his father's death, his mother's betrayal, losing his crown to the uncle who shared his mother's bed. With much prompting from me, he was putting these things behind him. But his father's murder …

'But how could your father have been murdered, my lord? The whole court saw him lie in state. I swear to you he had no wound on him, no bruise or cut.'

'He died of poison,' Hamlet said abruptly.

I shook my head. 'My lord, I dined with the king and queen that day. Your father ate what we all ate, drank from the jug that my father drank from too. Who could have poisoned him? How?'

'My uncle. Who else?' The bitterness in his voice could have shredded bark. 'My gracious uncle poured poison in my father's ear as he lay sleeping in the garden.'

Poison in the king's ear? I stared at him. It seemed more impossible than any story I had read in the library's books. Men died from the thrust of a spear, or a boar's tusks, or, yes, from poison in their food or drink. But in an ear? It was the stupidest way of poisoning someone I had ever heard of. How could Lord Claudius have known it would work?

'But ... that is impossible, my lord.'

'You do not think my uncle capable of murder? Such a villain, a smiling damned villain? You do not think a man can smile and smile and still be a villain?'

I almost expected the snow to steam around us at his heat.

'Is it impossible that my mother could marry her own brother-in-law, all for incestuous lust?' His eyes burned now. 'You think that not possible as well?'

'Please, my lord ...' I put my hand on his arm to quiet him.

The plot was too incredible to be true. Poison in an ear? And in the royal garden? What if a servant had looked out the door? Or a watchman had looked down from a tower? What excuse could Lord Claudius have given for pouring something into his brother's ear? Why not just slip mandrake into his wine, like those murderous Italian princes and princesses my father talked about?

I tried to work it out — sensibly, as my father's daughter should, not wild-eyed like this poor prince. Yes, I believed King Claudius capable of murder; just as his brother, Hamlet's own father, had cheated a king of his rightful kingdom. Neither were good men. But if Claudius had poured poison in the king's ear while he was sleeping, how did the ghost of the king know? He had been asleep. Did a ghost find out how he had died after his death?

And even if he did ... must a ghost tell the truth? I would not trust the old king to tell the truth about the colour of his stockings. Hamlet spoke of his father as having every virtue, and his mother as ruled only by her passions. But Queen Gertrude cared more for the kingdom than did either the old king or his brother. I might not know much about poison, or the ways of ghosts, but I did know the queen. It was not incestuous lust I had seen in her eyes, but love, and hope. And a priest had married them, just as that English king had married his dead brother's wife.

'Your mother deserves some happiness,' I ventured.

'Happy! Oh, happy harpy, steeped in the whorish sweat of her unseemly bed.'

I flushed at the image. Hamlet seemed more upset by his mother's marriage than the loss of the kingdom or his father's murder.

I stepped back, pulling my hand away. 'My lord ...'

He put his hands up to his face. They trembled as he pressed them to his eyes. 'The times are out of joint. Oh, cursed spite that ever I was sent to set them right.'

What had that ghost of bitterness and malice done to him? How could a father do this to his son?

'I have a plan,' he whispered.

'You won't tell everyone that your father's ghost told you he was murdered by his brother?' I asked anxiously.

No one would believe him, I thought. Not such a wild tale about poison in the king's ear. And even if people thought King Claudius was capable of murder — for, like me, they knew both men far better than this prince did — they would want to leave things as they were, at least for now, with Fortinbras's army still close enough to rampage across the land.

'The people will not support you till they know you,' I reminded him.

'I know. Wise Ophelia, is it any wonder that I love you?' He tried to smile at me, but it was as crooked as Yorick's back. 'No, I have another plan.'

His voice was too eager, excitement lurching out of sorrow. His eyes glittered now, like ice crystals in the trees. He was like a small boat, wind-tossed far from its harbour. I was anchored by a loving father, who was also father to the entire kingdom as its lord chancellor, and by a good brother. And a queen who treated me almost as a daughter.

I stepped close to him and took his hand again. 'Hamlet, please, be calm.' In my distress, I forgot to call him prince. 'It will all come right. The most important thing is that one day you will be king, no matter how your father died.'

'No! I am called to do a son's duty. "Remember me!" my father cried. How can I do nothing, and still live? I must wreak vengeance for him. But how can I prove a crime that no one saw?' He covered his face with his hands again. His words became sobs. 'Oh, that this too, too solid flesh would melt, or that the Almighty had not fixed his canon against self-slaughter.'

I stared at him, aghast. I had never realised the old king's true evil until now. What father would give his son such a burden that he'd rather die than carry it? Death did not make a bad man good. The king's ghost lied, I thought. He is as malicious dead as he was when he was alive. He hates that another should wear a crown, just as he envied King Fortinbras and stole his kingdom from him. And his son is the only tool he has for his revenge.

'Hamlet,' I began, but I had no words to comfort him.

I tugged at his hands. He dropped them from his face, and stared at me. His skin looked as white as the stream's ice.

'I must make my uncle admit his guilt.' His whisper was hoarse with anguish. 'But you must tell no one. No one! You must promise!'

'Of course I promise.'

'Oh, God!' He stared up at the grey unyielding sky. Snow hung among the clouds, ready to fall. We should go back. But this could not be talked about within the palace walls. Hamlet still stared up at the sky. 'How stale and weary is the world.'

What use were words now? I stood on tiptoe and kissed his cheek. It was the kind of kiss my nurse had given me.

He pulled me to him. I felt the warmth of his body through his velvet, through my fur. How was it I could not feel the cold, but could feel the heat of him?

He kissed me, in desperation at first, and then with something else. I had known kisses all my life, but none like this. It was … wet. He invaded me, like Fortinbras's army, marching across our border. I did not like it. But I did. When at last he pulled away, I panted like a fox running from the hounds. I wanted more …

This time I moved to him. His hands touched me, burning my breasts through the leather, fur and velvet. He pulled me down with him till I kneeled on the snow, his body pushing mine …

'Ophelia!'

I was so deep in passion it took moments to find myself again, to stumble to my feet. 'Laertes!' I blinked at my almost-stranger brother, his bearskin dark against the snow-clad trees, too dazed to say more.

'My lord.' Laertes bowed to Hamlet, coldly furious. 'I watched you leave the palace for the woods with my sister — alone. I thought perhaps you had lost your way. It has been so long since you have walked our land.'

Hamlet reached again for my hand. He pressed it once, then let it go. He too was panting. 'Not lost, I think, but found.'

I waited for him to claim the right to kiss me in the snow. As soon as he told my brother that we would be married, all would be well. Laertes would smile, and hug me, and kneel to Hamlet as his prince. I waited for his words.

The locket burned against my breast, with the same heat as his hands. A locket, not a ring. If Hamlet had meant to claim me as his wife here in the forest, why not a ring?

A crow called, triumphant, beyond the frozen stream. Perhaps it had found the beast's guts from the king's last hunt. Another answered it. Still Hamlet did not speak.

He has not claimed his kingdom, I thought, and nor has he claimed me now. And perhaps both were wise choices. Maybe Hamlet intended to ask my father's permission to marry me before he claimed me to my brother. He would have my help to sit upon a throne, and Laertes's and my father's, if only he would claim me.

Hamlet looked at the sky, then at the stream. He did not look at me.

Deep inside me, a small illusion broke. Hamlet had been born with a head to bear a crown, but did he have the stomach to be king?

Suddenly our love seemed to shrivel like a mushroom in the heat. So much wild talk — of murder, love and passion. How much was real? How much was shock and grief?

'Sister?' Laertes offered me his arm. 'It will be dark soon.' He glanced back at Hamlet. 'I would not have you lost among the snow.' I brushed the snow from my dress and took his arm numbly.

We walked through the woods in silence. Laertes lifted the branches for Hamlet to pass under, then me.

'I ... It is a fine day,' I said at last.

A foolish remark. I sounded like a child. Neither lover nor brother answered.

We reached the road. A carter with a load of turnips stopped so we could walk past him. Faces peered at us from farmhouses, and then from the market stalls. Curious faces, smiling. They had seen me walk into the forest with Prince Hamlet; now they saw my brother bringing me back.

All at once I was angry. What did Laertes, this brother who had so recently remembered he had a sister, think he was doing by humiliating me so? A man could love and kiss and even tumble in the hay, and no one thought anything of it. Laertes had baskets of lovers in Paris. Cartloads! I had heard Father questioning his servants. No doubt when he returned to Paris he would be at it again, like a spring bull among the cows.

No, my brother had it wrong. All would be well. I was no light-of-love! I was the lord chancellor's daughter. Hamlet had said he loved me. He would speak to Father today; and tomorrow the court would rejoice for us. Hamlet would dream of our marriage bed — I flushed, thinking of it too — not ghosts and poisoned ears.

We stepped up to our front door, Hamlet preceding us. I waited for Hamlet to ask leave to speak to my father.

He turned and bowed to me, then lifted my hand to kiss it. 'My lady, may this warm my soul until we meet again.'

'I ... I hope it does,' I said.

The footman opened the door for us. I waited for Hamlet to walk inside, so we could follow him. Instead, he turned and walked back across the courtyard towards the palace.

I stared after him, my skin as cold as it had been hot in the glade.

'Go to your room and change,' said Laertes softly. 'I will see you then.'

Gerda helped me remove the damp furs and silk, and dressed me afresh. I wished I could have warmed my mind as easily.

Why had Hamlet not spoken?

Perhaps he intended to seek out Father in the palace? Perhaps even now he was asking for my hand in marriage? But surely he could have said something — anything — to my brother, to assure him his intentions were honourable?

'I will go to see your father now.' That was all he had to tell Laertes. Or even, 'I will say more when your father has given me the right to claim you.'

But he'd said nothing. And a small space in my heart seemed empty too.

Chapter 10

I was dressed in lavender when I met Laertes in the corridor. He had changed as well, into his travelling clothes. He opened the door to our sitting room for me. I glanced at him. He didn't seem angry now, or not at me. He looked serious, with eyes of warning.

'My bags are packed,' he said. 'Write to me, with every ship the winds let sail.'

'Of course,' I said automatically.

I didn't know what to feel. I wanted to be furious, but I was grateful too. For I *had* forgotten myself out there in the snow with Hamlet.

'For Hamlet and the trifling of his favour ...' Laertes looked at me, as if he was trying to find the right words too. 'Hold it a toy in blood, sweet, not lasting. No more.'

I sank onto a cushion next to him. Hamlet had trusted me with his life's secrets, but I could not tell my brother that. 'No more than that?' My voice sounded like a mouse, hoping for cheese.

Laertes shook his head. 'Perhaps he loves you ... now.'

I opened my mouth to say he did. Laertes held up his hand. 'The safety and health of this whole kingdom depends on his choice. His will is not his own.'

His words blew the warmth from my limbs and heart. Laertes was right. How had I not seen it? Of all the girls in Denmark, I should have known that a prince cannot always choose his bride. How many times had my father told me of royalty's arranged marriages? Father had even planned a wedding for Hamlet, years ago, with a princess from England, though it had come to nothing when she died a child.

I was a suitable bride in peacetime. But what if Fortinbras changed his mind and invaded? Denmark would need allies. And this king and queen had only one son: one chance to ally with another house, to have another kingdom lend us armies.

Hamlet must know it too. Must also know that if he married a princess from England or the Low Countries, King Claudius would find it harder, even impossible, to disinherit him. Was that why he had not spoken back in the glade, was not speaking to my father now?

Laertes was still talking. I tried to listen, but my thoughts were too heavy to bear much more.

'You must weigh the loss of your honour if you listen to his songs, or lose your heart, or open your chaste treasure.'

I blinked. My chaste treasure? My brother thought I had tumbled in the snow with Hamlet; given him the first entry a husband would expect. Pig slops to you, dear brother! I thought. You do not know me. I had walked with Hamlet believing he would propose to me, kissed him because I believed he would ask to be my husband.

Laertes bent towards me, as stern as Nurse when I was four years old and had thrown my porridge down the privy. 'Fear it, Ophelia, fear it, my dear sister. Keep out of the danger of desire ... A maid is overgenerous enough if she unmasks her beauty to the moon ...'

My anger grew. Anger at myself — I had been a fool, had not seen that love may not lead to marriage. A green girl, dreaming of being queen. Anger at my brother too. Was Laertes my father to drone on and on like this? And how was I supposed to keep my beauty hidden from anyone but the moon, if I was a lady-in-waiting to the queen?

Buckets of pig slops, I thought. Why must I pretend I felt no passion, had not the wit to understand the kingdom, just because I wore a skirt, not hose? I sat with my hands in my lap, to stop them shaking.

Finally, his lecture drew to a close. I forced myself to smile sweetly. I chose my words carefully to show him that I too could use courtly speech, find a hundred words to decorate what could be said in half a dozen.

'I shall the effect of this good lesson keep as watchman to my heart. But, good my brother, do not, as some ungracious pastors do, show me the steep and thorny way to heaven while, like a puffed and reckless libertine, he himself the primrose path of dalliance treads.'

It was a speech worthy of our father, as long-winded as an autumn gale. Laertes looked at me, surprised. See, I thought, your little sister can spout words too. And sense.

Suddenly he grinned. 'Oh, fear me not!' And we were laughing — at each other, at ourselves. I knew that Laertes would still lift every skirt in Paris, if he could. And he knew that now I would not mistake a prince's passion for honourable love.

He hugged me, and I hugged him back: my warm and solid brother, Laertes, who did not see ghosts or talk of vengeance. And who, for all his dallying in Paris, had more wisdom than I, a girl who had wandered in the woods unchaperoned. He was right, and I had been wrong. And I forgave him for being right.

A footman opened the door. Father swept in, his ermine cloak almost touching the floor, in the fur-lined boots I had reminded his servants to make him wear, to stop the ache of his bones in the cold. I gazed at his expression, hoping that after all he had come to tell me Hamlet had asked for my hand.

No, that was not the face of a man who had given his daughter to a prince. His face was as watchful as if Fortinbras's army was below the castle.

Laertes stood. 'A double blessing is a double grace,' he said, and winked at me. Courtly words always pleased our father. 'Two parting speeches give more grace than one. Farewell, Ophelia, and remember well what I have said to you.'

I smiled back, realising that I would miss him. Indeed, it was good to have a brother.

'It is in my memory locked,' I promised him. 'And you yourself shall keep its key.'

'Farewell,' he said again. The footman opened the door for him, then shut it behind him.

Father looked at me sharply. 'What has he said to you?'

'So please you,' I said cautiously, 'something touching the Lord Hamlet.'

Father sat down heavily on the chair Laertes had just left. 'Well thought! I have just been told he has given private time to you, and you have been most free and bounteous.'

My last hope that Hamlet might have spoken to Father in the palace vanished. So Father was worried too. And, as was his way, would express it in a whole book of flowery words. I sat and watched my hands and waited for the words to pass.

At last he said, 'What is between you? Give me the truth.'

'He has made many tenders of his affection to me,' I said carefully, glad he did not know of the kisses in the snow.

'Affection? Pooh! You speak like a green girl. Do you believe his tenders, as you call them?'

'I do not know, my lord, what I should think,' I admitted.

Father, of all people, would know whether Hamlet might indeed marry me, or was bound to do his duty elsewhere.

'Then I must teach you! You are a baby to think these tenders are true coin. Tender yourself more dearly, or you will tender me a fool.'

Despair flooded me again. Father was right. I had been a fool. But I'd had reason to think that Hamlet was truly courting me. 'My lord, he importuned me with love in honourable fashion.'

Father snorted. 'Ay, fashion is a good word for it.'

'And he has given almost all the holy vows of heaven.' All except two, I thought: the two that mattered most. No vow to be betrothed to me; and no vow that made him my husband.

Father raised his hands as if speaking to the ceiling. 'Traps to catch unwary birdies! I know, when the blood burns, how generously the soul lends the tongue promises. But these blazes, daughter, give more light than heat.'

More words. Words and words and words. I'd had too many words today, and with too little substance — from Hamlet too. But at least my father's long speech gave me time to think. They did not know me, my father and my brother. All they saw was the girl, her clothes and manners, not the soul who lived beneath. I thought they didn't really know any woman, not truly. But they did know the ways of men, and nations. I had only been allowed the crumbs of knowledge that fell from their table.

Had Queen Gertrude felt like this married to Hamlet's

father, cut off from all but the crusts of Denmark's politics? Could she really have plotted with King Claudius, hoping for the life she had been denied, as girl and wife and mother?

No. I knew the queen. Even if she had dreamed of what might happen if she was free of the old king, she would not murder him. Nor did I think she'd be quiet if she suspected Claudius had. The ghost had lied. Or Hamlet had imagined the ghost, a figment of his grief. The whole plot was as fantastic as a play.

As fantastic as a girl who had dreamed she might be queen because a queen had smiled upon her, and a prince had murmured words of love. I had taken those smiles and words and put my own meaning on them. Father was right, under all those words. My dreams of being queen were no more real than Hamlet's nightmares of his father's ghost. Stupid, dreaming girl. How could I have thought myself so wise and been so foolish?

Father's speech was drawing to a close; I knew the signs. He looked at me now, not as if he was making a declaration to the council. 'I would not, in plain terms, from this time forth have you give words or talk with the Lord Hamlet.' He regarded me sternly. 'Look to it, I charge you.'

'I shall obey, my lord,' I said, and bowed my head, a dutiful daughter. And, one day perhaps, if I could repair my reputation now, some man's dutiful wife. But not a princess, nor a queen.

I felt as empty as a sausage casing when it has been emptied of its meat, and as useless.

Chapter 11

I did not sleep that night. Nor did I go to my tower on the battlements, where the ghost had bred my foolish hopes. Had King Fortinbras been trying to revenge himself on the House of Hamlet through me?

No. My ghost had been a good man, who had made one mistake. Nor had he ordered me to try to become queen. I had done that myself.

I turned restlessly in my bed cabinet. Did Hamlet love me? Yes, I thought so. But perhaps he thought that as the lord chancellor's daughter, I would know he was not free to marry me, with Denmark under threat of invasion, and his own position so uncertain. He must have thought me willing to give myself to him for love; not just my body, but my reputation and my life. He could not know that a ghost had once given me a dream of being a queen.

Or perhaps, in his anguish, he had thought more of himself than me. My heart settled like a lump of butter in a bucket of whey.

Hamlet believed what he wanted to believe. Claudius

had stolen his crown and his mother. Hamlet would have been all too willing to believe the ghost's lies.

And they must be lies. Queen Gertrude might love unwisely — *had* loved unwisely; she had told me so — but she had lived with that love for twenty-six years and kept her virtue. Nor could I blame her for taking the throne with Fortinbras threatening the kingdom. Her hand was steadier than Hamlet's would have been; as was King Claudius's. The queen had saved Denmark from invasion. A woman like that would not kill her husband, nor her king.

The ghost had lied. Or jealously imagined himself betrayed by his brother and wife, who still had the gift of happy life. Whichever it was, it was done from malice, not from love. Hamlet had been a fool to trust him. And I a fool to trust Hamlet …

I dozed at last; and in the morning let Gerda dress me. I even ate a slice of toasted cheese. I waited for a messenger to call me to attend the queen, as usual. But no one came.

At last, I took myself to the stillroom. Better to do something than sit brewing the same thoughts over and over. If you cook hops more than once, they lose their strength. Thoughts thought too much grow weak too.

The footman came while I was simmering a tonic for a maid with the flux: rose heps and dried mint in barley water with a little chamomile.

The footman bowed. 'My lady, Prince Hamlet waits for you below.'

Every doubt rose in me again. I wanted to see him; longed to see him, despite what he had cost me. Hamlet needed me. He also needed my loyalty, advice, a steady mind. But Father had forbidden me to see him. I had caused too much gossip already and possibly damaged my father's position at court, and certainly my own. What husband would want the prince of Denmark's leftovers?

I had to choose: my father's will, or Hamlet's. And it must be Father's. I could trust Father's love for me. I could not trust the prince's.

I thrust away an image of Hamlet's anguished face, the memory of his skin on mine. I tried to call up anger instead. Hamlet had as good as abandoned me there in the forest, I told myself again, failing to claim me before my brother, turning love to shame. He had called me his wise counsel, but I had not been wise. At heart, I had still been six years old, dreaming of playing princes and queens. Hamlet was older than I; he knew the world. I might be a wise sixteen, but I had walked innocently into the woods yesterday. He had not.

I lifted my chin. 'Please tell His Highness that, with all deference, I cannot see him.' I gestured at the pan on the fire. 'I have duties I must attend to.'

The footman bowed. 'My lady.'

Twenty flickers of the candle and he was back. 'My lady, Prince Hamlet asks *when* it might suit you to see him?'

'Please give him my most loyal regards, as befits … um …' I tried to find the right words. 'As befits Denmark's most loyal servant. But I cannot see him. Simply that.'

The footman stared. One does not dismiss a prince.

'Go,' I told him. He left.

As soon as he was gone, I wished I hadn't said it. I dared to do so much that my father did not know. Why did I not have courage to see Hamlet? Just see him, that was all. Advise him. Make it clear I could be a friend, but not a mistress.

But that would mean disobeying Father, and in his own house. And each time Hamlet called here, there would be more gossip. Gossip breeds gossip, like a marsh breeds midges.

I took the pan off the fire. If only I had a mother to ask for advice, or a friend. It was impossible to speak of Hamlet's desperation and its cause to Lady Annika, Lady Anna or Lady Hilda, much less to the queen.

The queen. Had she failed to call for me today because she too had heard the gossip that I had vanished into the forest alone with her son?

I took a deep breath. Prince Hamlet had his friend Horatio to keep him steady. He had even told me he had a plan, though I had let passion take over before he shared it with me.

I could not risk shaming my father further. Father had given his whole life to guiding Denmark and its kings. A scandal between his daughter and the heir to the throne might lose Father not just his reputation but his position here at court.

My night wanderings up the tower were possible only because no one knew of them. If only I had been as discreet with Hamlet. I had been proud, thinking people would say: 'There goes the girl who will be queen.' Instead, they had whispered, 'There goes the prince's new light-of-love.'

I clenched my fists. Hamlet, who was older than I and knew so much more about the world, had not thought of me. To take me out without a chaperone, with all the eyes of Denmark on us. To kiss me like that, in the snow ... I touched my lips. I could feel the kiss again, feel its warmth in my body.

I rubbed my lips hard, to take away the memory. I had to trust the wisdom of my father and my brother. I had to tell Prince Hamlet, 'No.'

The days passed. The sun rose earlier each morn. Gradually the air smelled of mud and flowers, not of snow and tin and ice. We drank in the sunlight like a kitten laps up milk. Still I did not speak to Prince Hamlet. Nor did the queen call for me to attend her. She had been the object of murmurings about her own affairs; she did not need to add to the gossip with whispers about me and Hamlet. Her Majesty had given me leave to walk with her son, but not to dance about the trees of the forest, to leave my maid behind and go unchaperoned. Perhaps the queen too thought me shameless.

I tried to dull the pain with duty. The spring's sunlight showed the winter cobwebs. I ordered every corner of the house swept. Every carpet was taken out and aired and beaten; every pane of glass was polished with vinegar and soft cloths. My duty was in this household, and here I stayed. I did not even visit my tower at night.

Safe among the dishcloths and cheeses of home, Hamlet's declaration that the king had been murdered seemed more and more absurd. Kings died in battle; or, if they were poisoned, it was slipped into their wine at a banquet, as was done in Rome or Venice, and their dying agony was witnessed by all the court. Our king had died napping in the sunshine in his garden. How was it possible to poison an ear? Except, I thought, with malice. Or with careless words of love, like those that had so damaged me.

I inspected the household linens; engaged a woman to darn the frayed edges; had my father's cuffs re-whitened; wrote out the household accounts in my neatest hand for him to inspect. I looked at the pages and tried to smile: I had done well. Only half of the house allowance had been spent. A wise housewife filled her cellars for winter from summer's plenty, rather than buy salt pork, dried fish or cheese at high winter prices. We still had good supplies of salted butter, along with cheeses that would mature for next year or the year after. A good cheese grows more valuable the longer it spends in the cellar.

This is all I can ever hope for now, I thought: to tend my father's household well; and, perhaps, one day, a husband's.

I did not go marketing in case the sight of me revived the gossip. I saw no one, except Father and the servants. Even Father stopped telling me the news of court at breakfast. Perhaps he thought that he had given me ideas above my station. Never had I been such a dutiful daughter. Never had I felt as though chains hung from my wrists and ankles, and I would never get them loose.

Prince Hamlet did not come to our house again. But his letters did, one each day, handed by a palace servant discreetly to Gerda at the marketplace, sealed with the prince's imprint. They were letters of love, of loneliness, of longing. I tried to tell myself that he had made an image of me, as he had of his dead father. It was the image he loved, not me. If he truly loved me, he had only to speak to my father, to claim me as a husband should. He didn't. Yet my heart bled with every page.

A dutiful daughter would show her father every letter. I did not. I had so little now, just these crumbs of love. Letters could not be gossiped about if no one saw them. And if I did not reply, Gerda would not gossip either — or, at least, not about me.

But she brought me gossip from the market, and I swallowed it hungrily, eager to hear about the world beyond our door. The barrel-maker's apprentice wanted to marry. Who had heard of such a thing, a lad not yet a journeyman thinking he could marry? Someone had planted snowdrops on the grave of the poor girl who had drowned herself and her unborn babe. Was it the man who had ruined her? Were the flowers of guilt or love? Lady Anna had a new cloak trimmed with bearskin, which had given her an itch. Everyone knew, said Gerda smugly, that bearskin was too coarse for a lady's skin.

At last, as the flies arrived with the first warm breeze, Father began to speak again of court affairs at breakfast. There was to be a new tax on French wine instead of on dried fish — the queen's suggestion, said my father. It was a tax the rich could afford, which did not hurt the poor. The king of Norway was paying Fortinbras a large sum of money to attack Poland with his army.

'There is no danger of Prince Fortinbras invading now,' Father said cheerfully, peering at me over his cold veal chop and mustard. 'A firm hand and firm mind, and the kingdom is kept straight.'

I nodded. 'Yes, Father.'

I thought: he has not said, 'The palace is gossiping that King Claudius murdered his brother.' Perhaps Father would think gossip like that unsuitable for his daughter's ears. But Gerda hadn't brought back a tale like that either.

The palace bred gossip as a bearskin breeds fleas. If Lord Claudius had poured poison in the king's ear, if he had even been in the garden, surely someone on one of the towers would have seen him? If there is no gossip, even among the servants, I thought, it cannot be true.

If only Hamlet could accept that too.

Chapter 12

The first day of summer blew gusts of snow, as if the year laughed at us for trying to keep it confined to a calendar, and white tops on the harbour's waves. It brought a letter from Hamlet too, the first in a week. I had begun to think he had let me go. But these pages were delivered by a footman from the palace an hour after Father had left me, instead of thrust into Gerda's hands more discreetly in the marketplace, and were waxed with the prince's seal.

I wondered how many people knew already that Prince Hamlet had sent a letter to the Lady Ophelia this morning, and to her own hand, not through her father as was proper.

I thanked the footman and waited till he had left the room. Then I broke the seal and unfolded the pages. The prince wrote in a scholar's script: the writing gracious, but hurried today and smudged, as if he had not paused to blot his words.

To the celestial, and my soul's idol, the most beautified Ophelia …

Beautified, I thought; celestial. I am neither of those things. I am a girl who knows her country and cheese. Then I read the words below. My heart stopped, then began to beat again. I heard his voice in every word.

Doubt thou the stars are fire;
Doubt that the sun doth move;
Doubt truth to be a liar;
But never doubt I love.

Oh dear Ophelia, I am ill at these numbers. I have not art to reckon my groans: but that I love thee, oh most best, believe it. Adieu. Thine evermore, most dear lady, while this machine is in him, Hamlet.

The locket he had given me burned against my skin. I did not doubt his love. But his love could scorch me, like the fiery stars. It had already blackened my name.

Nor did I doubt his pain.

If I'd had no father, I would have gone to Hamlet then. Would have cast all away to make him smile, as I had before.

I tucked the letter into my bodice. It felt cold at first, until my body warmed it. Warm as the locket, next to my heart. Another letter like that and I doubted I would have the strength to stay away.

By midday, the snow had gone. The sky hung as blue as if it had never tasted a cloud, the sun straining once again to reach the topmost sky.

Doubt that the sun doth move ...

The image clutched me. I couldn't shake it off.

I climbed up to the attic to check that the winter furs were guarded against the moths. From the top window, I saw fields green with barley stretched like a green carpet to the horizon. On the other side, pigs rooted under the oak trees, hoping for acorns left uneaten from last autumn. Hares would duck and run in the forest, and deer too. Last summer, I would have called Gerda and a footman and we'd have gone berrying, or gathered mushrooms under the trees. Not now. Not till the gossips' tongues had quietened.

When the queen calls for me again, I thought, I shall know that I have been redeemed.

Perhaps she never would.

Stop it, I told myself. Stop sighing for the moon.

Doubt truth to be a liar, the wind whispered at the window.

Something about the letter niggled me. *But never doubt I love.* Why should I doubt him? I didn't doubt his love, only his ability to love me honourably, as a wife, not a prince's mistress. Surely he realised that now.

Doubt thou the stars are fire ... It was almost as if the letter held a hidden message, not just telling me he loved me and always would — a small sword stabbed my heart at the thought — but saying something else, in words that no one else might understand. But what?

I sat on a chest of old linen. I went through the poem in my mind, the words that followed it. Each was blazed on my mind now. But if there was a hidden message, I couldn't see it.

Stop thinking about it, I told myself. Stop thinking of Hamlet too, of dreams and kisses. Think of cheese instead. Cheese was sensible, dependable. I could never have the moon, but I did have cheeses: three score of them, all sealed in wax; and the shelves freshly scrubbed for the first spring cheeses from our estates. I had a storeroom full of linen; a feather bed that smelled of sunlight and lavender. I had a father who kept me safe from harm. I was one of the most fortunate girls in the whole kingdom and I should remember it.

And I had my father's cuffs to embroider if I had nothing better to do. I took a last look at the cows munching the new green grass that turned the sunlight into cheese, then headed downstairs. Placid obedient cows, just like a well-mannered daughter.

I had already finished one cuff. I looked at it critically. It was good work, good enough for the king's lord chancellor. No one would ever say, 'Ah, look at Lord Polonius's cuffs, so cunningly embroidered.' But they would notice if his cuffs were unadorned. I began on the next, stitching a row of small flowers, and then our family's crest: two deer upright against a shield. White thread on white cloth so it spoke of carefulness, not boasting ... Someone screamed below. A maid has seen a mouse, I thought. I must tell Gerda to put out cheese mixed with henbane ...

'My lady.' The footman panted at the door. 'My lady, please, you must come!'

'What is it?' Had the cook set the kitchen on fire?

'It's Prince Hamlet.'

'I … Please tell him I cannot see him.'

The footman looked at me imploringly. 'My lady, I dare not. Please see him.'

'My father —'

'John has gone to fetch Lord Polonius.'

I could not understand why the man was so urgent. To be sure, it was a great thing to turn a prince away from the door, but I had done so often by now.

'Give Prince Hamlet my most deferential regards,' I began.

Footsteps pounded up the stairs. And there was Hamlet. Not a prince today, just a man. But I had never seen any man like this, except the mad beggar who had capered by the church one summer, asking for alms. Hamlet's careful black garb was gone. He wore only a white shirt, its buttons all undone, showing his chest. Red stockings hung below his knees. I had never seen a man's bare legs before. Had never realised they were so hairy.

I stood, putting the cuff and needle to one side. I forced my hands and voice to be calm. 'My lord,' I began.

I stopped as he staggered across the room to me, his face so twisted I should hardly have known him. He grabbed my hand.

'My lord, please. You are hurting me!' I tried to pull away.

Still he did not speak. Instead, he stared into my eyes as a child might look into a well, to see if there is a water sprite hidden in its depths.

'Please, my lord. Tell me what is wrong.'

And yet I knew it even as I spoke. Knew his anguish. Knew the burden that he carried, the evil whisperings of his father's ghost. Knew his love too. And that I had spurned him when he needed me so desperately, when I had been perhaps his only true friend at court.

'Hamlet,' I said softly, 'my lord, I am sorry.'

I reached my hand towards him. I had no thought of my honour now, or my father's, or my lost dreams of being queen. I would throw away all I had just to ease his pain.

Too late. I didn't think he even heard me.

He grabbed my hand, stared at it in disgust, then thrust it away, like a man throwing away a stick he had found to be a snake. He staggered from the room.

I ran to the window, and watched him run from our front door, towards the palace. Then I sat and cried.

And then, carefully, I wiped my eyes and prepared to tell my father.

My father told the king and queen, of course, as a good lord chancellor should. I waited at our house, as I had when I was a child and expected a scolding. At least then I had known it would be bread and water for supper. What punishment would come my way for this?

I could not even sew. I sat, and thought of Hamlet. At last, I heard my father's tread on the stairs, slow and heavy.

I stood to greet him. 'Father?'

He nodded at me sombrely. 'I have told Their Majesties, and shown them the letters that he sent. They think as I do.'

'What is that?' I whispered.

'That Prince Hamlet is mad for love.'

I heard the whisper in the breeze down the chimney: *Doubt truth to be a liar; but never doubt I love.*

I could not think. I could not feel. I had done this to him. I had offered friendship to the friendless; given love to one who had lost a father, a kingdom, even a mother too. Then I had snatched it from him just as his burden grew too great to bear alone. I shook my head, trying not to cry. I should have explained to him. Told him I loved him still, but must obey my father.

Had I loved him, truly? If I did, could I have hurt him so easily? Had I been more in love with a dream throne, and removed myself from him once my dream had been taken from me?

'Father? What will happen to him?' I had heard of mad wretches being locked in towers, chained to the walls so they did not harm themselves or their attendants, and screaming away their lives. I did not think I could bear it if that happened to Hamlet.

'Their Majesties will act with majesty, high ends and higher heart. He will be cared for. But, daughter, they must care for a whole kingdom, not just a son.'

Which was no true answer, only words. Father had so many words, gathered during a lifetime at court, where true feelings must be concealed behind the right words.

Suddenly I wasn't sure I trusted the king — nor even the queen — to care well for Hamlet. Even without his ghostly father's claims, they had robbed him of so much already. Would they take his freedom too?

'Father ...' I sought my words carefully. 'Could there be another reason for the prince's state?'

He looked at me, suddenly a chancellor, not just a father. 'Why do you ask that?'

'Sir, his father's death has hurt him greatly. And he is ... in distress at ... what has happened since.'

I felt I was picking the good grains out of a sack of mouldy rice in order to make a pudding. Even to my father I could not say, 'Hamlet's uncle stole his mother and his crown. I do not know which he grieves for most.' Of all the people in the kingdom, I could not tell my father that. Nor could I hint that Hamlet believed the new king to be a murderer. My father must be loyal to the king. My words would be treason.

Father said nothing for a moment, then murmured, 'Daughter, truly I do not know.' He looked out the window. 'When I was young, I suffered from love, almost like this.'

I stared. I knew Father had loved my mother too much to leave the home she had made and move into the palace. But to love her to the point of madness? My sedate and careful father, with his strings of words?

The moment passed. Father looked at me again with chancellor's eyes. 'I have watched the young man. He speaks to me like one deranged, and to his old friends too — young Rosencrantz and Guildenstern.'

'He has friends come to Elsinore?'

I hoped he had more friends here than just Horatio, who, after all, had been the one to tell him of his father's ghost.

'Old friends from his childhood. The king has called them here.'

My hope walked out of the room. These so-called friends would be allies of the king. My father was still talking, as if puzzling the matter out. He too suspected Hamlet's madness did not spring only from lost love. Love may have fanned the fire, but it had not lit the flames.

'I heard him speak with all good accent and discretion due a prince to a group of players come to Elsinore.' Father's voice was careful.

'Players?'

'Actors. A travelling troupe. He knew them at Wittenberg, and bade me see them well-bestowed and comfortable. A princely act. And yet,' Father shook his head, 'when he had the master player speak a speech, he lost his colour. I saw tears in his eyes.'

'What was the speech?' I asked quietly.

'A matter most properly said, with noble words, concerning the revered ancient Priam, slain most treacherously by Pyrrhus. The part that moved him was when Hecuba, Priam's wife, comes upon her husband's body as Pyrrhus hacks at it with his sword.' Father shrugged. 'What is he to Hecuba, or Hecuba to him, that he should weep for her? And yet the prince said ...' Father frowned. 'He said his madness is only north-north-west.

When the wind is southerly, he knows a hawk from a handsaw. Sometimes I think that though it be madness, there may be method in it. Their Majesties must be sure that this sad feeling comes from love of you, not from … other causes.'

I nodded. A prince who was mad from righteous anger at having lost his throne might try to raise an army. It would be a hopeless cause, unless he had some of the great houses at his side, but still dangerous — for both Their Majesties and for the realm.

'How can they tell what has caused his … madness?' It was hard for me even to say the word.

My father stood. 'You must come to the palace. Sit in the hall reading. We will watch from behind the tapestries to see what Prince Hamlet says to you.'

I sat silent. Was this a trap? Was the king trying to make my father a witness should Hamlet speak treason? If Hamlet claimed the king had married adulterously, much less murdered his brother, the king could have him executed.

I thought of Hamlet's head laid on the block, the axeman's sword slashing down. Three years ago, the old king had had a lord executed just for singing a song when he was drunk about a man who cheated another of his lands. The head had stood on a pike all summer for the crows to eat; and its bare skull had watched us all the winter.

I shivered. A daughter must do her father's will. A subject must obey her king and queen. At least if I went to the palace, I could see Hamlet, speak to him. Perhaps undo some of the harm I had caused. I could make sure I stopped him saying anything treasonous.

I nodded. 'I will do your bidding.'

Chapter 13

I had Gerda dress me carefully: a blue silk petticoat, so dark it might almost be mourning, pale blue sleeves and overskirt. No jewellery except the locket — against the cloth of my dress this time, so Hamlet would see it, would understand that by wearing it I declared he was still next to my heart.

I walked with Father across the courtyard. No connecting door and passage today. The world should see me come to the palace. Did I imagine people pointing, whispering? 'See how her father makes sure she doesn't stray today,' they'd say. I looked straight ahead.

Over the drawbridge we went, and into the great hall. Servants bowed, as they had always done. At least there were no whispers — or not till we had passed.

Up the stairs, past the petitioners waiting to see Their Majesties, and into the receiving room. The king and queen sat side by side on their thrones. Lady Annika, Lady Hilda and Lady Anna sat on their stools as usual. The embroidered whiskers of Lady Annika's hound were still unfinished. Did I imagine a faint smile as she saw me? But if there was a smile of welcome, it vanished almost immediately. She bent her head again to her embroidery.

The king and queen made no sign they had noticed us. We stood while they considered petitions from two farmers arguing about who should have the water from a stream: he who owned the land where the spring rose from the ground; or he who owned the land the water flowed across — except his neighbour had diverted it all to clean his cow byre. It seemed such a simple matter, too easily solved to bother a king. But I knew from my father that a ruler's days were made up of such small things.

The king looked bored. I wondered how long he would bother to consider affairs of state like these. The old king had mostly left them to my father.

King Claudius waved a hand wearily at the two farmers standing so earnestly in their cleaned leathers and work boots. 'Gertrude? What do you say?'

The queen smiled at the men. 'With your permission, my lord, I give this judgment. That the owner of the spring shall take no more than half the water at any one time, and his neighbour shall have access to the other half. And he who took the water and left his neighbour with none shall give a dinner which both families will attend. There will be ale, and dancing, and both shall shake the hand of friendship across the table.'

The farmers bowed. Neither looked especially happy, but not unhappy either. The judgment, perhaps, would work.

'Well thought,' muttered Father. 'Her Majesty has a man's mind along with the dignity of a queen.'

The queen caught my father's eye. She whispered to the king, who stood.

'We will hear the other petitioners anon,' he said. 'Chancellor, will you and your daughter walk with us?'

I curtseyed deeply as they approached. How would the queen treat me with the whole court looking on? To my relief, I saw her hand extended. I kissed it as I stood up.

'We have missed you, child,' she said.

I glanced at her, and saw that she knew my relief. I had been afraid of her anger — anger that Hamlet was distraught because of me; or that a lady of hers had risked her reputation, and with her son too.

Once again, I almost loved her. I looked at her, tall and gracious, her hand now on King Claudius's arm. Impossible that she could have been part of a plot to pour poison in her husband's ear; that she could take her son's kingdom and give it to his uncle simply for lust. This was a good woman, who acted from good motives. And yet her actions had still lost her son his throne, and possibly his mind.

We walked behind Their Majesties, down a corridor. I did not ask where we were going. At last, the footmen opened the doors into the library.

I glanced around; my friends, the books, gazed back at me. I had missed them, even more than I had missed Her Majesty's favour and the world outside our house.

Two young men stood as we entered, then bowed low. They were Hamlet's age, dressed in what had been high fashion five years ago. Now, their shoes were too long, their hats the wrong shape, one in too bright a yellow, the other in clashing pinks.

'Good Rosencrantz, kind Guildenstern,' murmured the queen.

The king beckoned them. 'You have seen Prince Hamlet?'

'We have, Your Majesty,' said the one in pink, bowing again so the feather in his hat scraped the floor.

'And can you get from him why he puts on this confusion, grating all his days with dangerous lunacy?'

Dangerous indeed, I thought. If they say he is dangerous, he will be locked up; not just his kingdom lost, but all his world.

'He does confess he feels himself distracted,' said the one in yellow. 'But from what cause he will not speak.'

'He stays away from us,' said the one in pink. He sounded affronted. 'And with a crafty madness keeps aloof when we would bring on him some confession of his true state.'

Spoken in true courtly flowery fashion, I thought, like a dog licking the king's boots. No wonder Hamlet would have none of these friends.

'Did he receive you well?' asked the queen quietly.

'Most like a gentleman,' said the one in yellow.

'But with much forcing of his disposition,' said the one in pink.

'Niggard of question; but of our demands, most free in his reply,' said Yellow.

'Did you see him with any ... pastime?' asked the queen.

I looked at her sharply. Was she wondering if Hamlet was, after all, sounding out the loyalty of other lords?

Yellow smiled, and nodded. 'Madam, he has ordered certain players to put on a play for him tonight.'

My father stepped forward. 'It is most true. And he beseeched me to entreat Your Majesties to hear and see it.'

King Claudius smiled. I thought I saw a tinge of relief too.

'With all my heart,' he said. 'It makes me most content to hear this. Good gentlemen, drive him on to these delights.'

I was relieved too. There could be no harm in a play. And it might remind Hamlet of Wittenberg and his contentment there.

Pink and Yellow bowed so low they might have swept the palace floor.

'We shall, my lord,' said Yellow.

They left, and the king turned to his wife. 'Sweet Gertrude, leave us too. We have sent for Hamlet. Lady Ophelia's father and I will wait here, hidden, so we may judge if his affliction comes from love.'

The queen inclined her head. 'I shall obey you.' She held out her hand for me to kiss, as if there had been no awkwardness between us. 'And for your part, Ophelia,

I do wish that your good beauty be the happy cause of Hamlet's wildness.'

I looked at her doubtfully.

She smiled at me. A true smile. 'I hope your virtues will bring him to his former way, to both your honours.'

I curtseyed again. 'Madam, I wish it may.'

My heart burned. 'To both your honours' — what did she mean? Was she suggesting that if I could soothe Hamlet out of madness, she might allow our marriage? I tried to stop my thoughts dancing with the moonbeams. Just speak to him, I told myself. Comfort him. Make sure he says nothing that is treasonous.

I thrust away the image of the rotting skull on the pike. I would not see Hamlet there, traitor's food for crows.

My father talked. I didn't listen. I took a book, any book, from the far shelves.

The library doors opened. I stood back, in the shadows. The king and my father slipped behind a tapestry hanging on the wall.

Hamlet was dressed in black again. This time his shirt was buttoned, his stockings up, but he wore no hat. His hair had not been attended to since I had seen him last. It looked rough as a rat's nest.

I had hoped Hamlet would look across the library and see me. But he crossed to the window and stared out. 'To be, or not to be — that is the question,' he murmured to the clouds. He shook his head. 'Is it nobler in the mind to suffer the slings and arrows of outrageous fortune, or to take arms against a sea of troubles and, by opposing, end them?'

I froze. Was Hamlet talking about an uprising against the king? I had to stop him. I stepped forward as he continued his conversation with the sky.

'To die: to sleep, no more; to end the heartache and the thousand natural shocks that flesh is heir to. It is a consummation devoutly to be wished.' He closed his eyes, as if he could feel that final sleep already. 'To die, to sleep ...'

I stopped as suddenly as if a tree root had snaked up and bound me to the floor. Hamlet spoke of suicide, not rebellion. Was this the man I had loved? I ached with pity for him.

'To sleep: perchance to dream.' Hamlet grimaced. 'Yes, there's the rub! For in that sleep of death what dreams may come, when we have shuffled off this mortal coil. Why else bear the horror of so long a life? Who would bear the whips and scorns of time, the oppressor's wrong, the proud man's humiliation, the pangs of despised love, when he himself might his final end make with a bare bodkin?'

I clutched my book to me. I could not bear to hear him talk of killing himself with a dagger. But his anguish so filled the room I could not move.

'Who would bear this load, to grunt and sweat under a weary life, but for the dread of something after death, the undiscovered country from where no traveller returns?' He shook his head at the sky. 'Thus conscience does make cowards of us all, and thus the native hue of resolution is made sallow with the pale cast of thought, and enterprises of great pith and moment turn awry, and lose the name of action.'

Enterprises of great pith and moment — did he mean armed rebellion? I did not know. Who could pluck sense from that great flow of words? But I could not risk what he might say next. My feet found strength and I stepped forward.

He turned, and saw me. I hoped he would come to me. He didn't. He stood by the window, its light so bright it was hard to read his face.

'Soft you now,' he said quietly. 'The fair Ophelia.' His voice grew bitter. 'Nymph, in thy prayers be all my sins remembered.'

I tried to keep my voice steady, tried not to look at the tapestry where my father and the king hid. 'Good my lord, how has your honour been this many a day?'

He gave a slight bow, as if we were strangers. 'I humbly thank you. I am well, well, well.'

I touched the locket at my heart. 'My lord, I have remembrances of yours that I have longed long to return. I pray you, will you take them now?'

He turned his back to me and stared out the window. 'No, not I. I never gave you aught.'

Words came to me then; courtly words, words you should say to a prince, especially when your father and a king are listening. 'My honoured lord, you know right

120

well you did, and with them words of so sweet breath composed as made the things more rich.'

He heard the sincerity in my voice. His face softened.

I tried to smile at him. 'Their perfume lost, take these again; for to the noble mind, rich gifts are poor when givers prove unkind.' I fumbled at the locket and held it out to him. 'There, my lord.'

He almost smiled as he stepped towards me.

A rat scratched at the skirting board. No, not a rat — a man's dagger, rubbing against the wall. My eyes darted to the tapestry where Father and the king hid.

Hamlet followed my glance. Saw the tapestry bulge, just for a moment, with a man's shape. He looked back at me, his face suddenly midwinter. 'Ha! Are you honest?'

I hesitated. If I told him openly that the king was behind the tapestry, I would be guilty of treason too. 'My lord?'

'Are you fair?'

'What means your lordship?' I looked at him imploringly, begging him silently not to betray us both.

'That if you be honest and fair, your honesty should admit no discourse to your beauty.'

I clutched my book in relief. We were back to court speech, playing with words. I could do that too. Safe words, which would not get him killed.

'Could beauty, my lord, have better commerce than with honesty?'

'Yes. For beauty will rather transform honesty into a bawd than honesty can make beauty honest too. This was once a paradox, but now we have proof.'

He gazed at me. I bit my lip. He was playing with words indeed, but his meaning was all too clear. Hamlet knew that I was betraying him. My part in this plot had snatched away his last faith in me.

'I did love you once,' he said abruptly.

My voice was a butterfly caught in a gale as I answered. 'Indeed, my lord, you made me believe so.'

'You should not have believed me. A family like mine does not breed truth. I loved you not.'

The old library walls creaked around us, as summer's sun warmed the stones. *Doubt that the sun doth move*, I thought, *but never doubt I love.*

I whispered, 'I was the more deceived.'

I held my hand out to him again. I tried to make my face say what my voice could not: that I cared for him, would help him, if I could.

He whirled away from me. 'Get thee to a nunnery!' His voice was harsh, with a depth of bitter rage I had never heard before. 'Why would you be a breeder of sinners?'

I stared at him, unable to answer.

He grimaced. 'I am myself indifferent honest, yet I could accuse me of such things that it were better my mother had not borne me. I am proud, revengeful, ambitious, with more offences at my beck than I have thoughts to put them in, imagination to give them shape, or time to act them. What should such fellows as I do, crawling between earth and heaven? We are arrant knaves all; believe none of us. Go thy ways to a nunnery.'

Something rustled behind me, cloth against cloth. I dared not look around. Was it the king, or my father? Had Hamlet heard it too?

He had. He looked at the tapestry, then at me. 'Where is your father?' His voice changed. His speech before seemed aimed as much at the universe as me. This question was soft, and sharp as a rapier.

I hesitated. 'At home, my lord.' What else could I say, with Father and the king listening?

He knew I lied. Whatever he had thought of me before, he knew for certain now he couldn't trust me.

He spoke to the tapestry. 'Let the doors be shut upon him that he may play the fool nowhere but in his own house!' he said harshly. And then to me: 'Farewell.'

'Oh, help him, sweet heavens!' I whispered.

Hamlet made towards the door. I thought he would leave me, when he turned again, his face twisted. 'If you do marry, I give you this plague for your dowry. Even if you are as chaste as ice, as pure as snow, you shall not escape!'

He came towards me so furious I stepped back. I had seen his father strike a serving wench while wearing this same black face of anger. Would Hamlet hit me too?

'Get thee to a nunnery,' he repeated. He kept coming, his slow pace more frightening than any rush. 'Or if you have to marry, marry a fool. Wise men know too well what monsters you make of us.'

I cowered back as he raised his hand. His voice rose to a scream. 'To a nunnery, go! And quickly too!'

I lifted my arm to stop his blow.

He looked at his hand as if surprised to see it raised, and lowered it. 'Farewell,' he said again, and once more turned to go.

I shut my eyes and prayed aloud. 'Oh, heavenly powers, restore him!'

He stood at the door again as if he could not leave, his voice low and bitter, each word striking me in the face. It was as if a chain kept pulling him back, to hit me with yet more words. 'I have heard of your paintings too. God has given you one face and you make yourselves another.'

I shook my head. I had never painted my face. My only lie to him had been what I had not said.

'You jig, you amble, you lisp; you nickname God's creatures and make your wantonness your ignorance.' He spoke to me, but I wasn't sure he even saw me. 'Go to, I'll no more of it!'

I tried not to sob. Father and the king would hear if I cried now. I tried to think of something — anything — that might soften Hamlet's fury. But what did I have to say? For I *had* betrayed him, this man who had given me his love. I had taken his love to feed my dream of being queen, but hadn't had the strength to give him fair return.

He stared at me, his voice quiet now. 'It has made me mad. I say we will have no more marriages. Those who are married already — all but one — shall live. The rest shall stay as they are. To a nunnery, go.'

He turned on his heel. The door slammed behind him.

I clutched my book. He wanted me to go to a nunnery? No. I had betrayed Hamlet to be a dutiful daughter. That must be my punishment: to stay a daughter, till I died.

And what of Hamlet? If I had lost, he had lost much more. A noble mind so lost to madness. He had been scholar, courtier, the hope of Denmark. All now gone.

And I, dejected and wretched, had drunk the honey of his music vows. Now I must see this — a prince's reason — like sweet bells jangled, out of tune and harsh.

'Woe is me,' I whispered, 'to have seen what I have seen, to see what I see.'

The tapestry was flung aside in a small shower of dust. I caught the scent of mouse droppings.

'His affections do not tend towards love,' the king said. 'And what he said, though it lacked form, was not madness. He is brooding on something else. Plotting, perhaps.'

I did not like King Claudius, but no one could say he was a fool.

He looked at Father. 'I have decided to send the prince to England, to present its king with a tribute from our country. It is my hope that the voyage, the change of country, will make him forget whatever he is planning. What do you think?'

'It shall do well,' said Father obediently. When had Father ever said no to a king? He looked at me, then back to the king. 'Yet do I believe his grief comes only from neglected love.'

Was Father trying to keep Hamlet in Denmark? Or keep him safe from suspicion of treason? Father couldn't know the depth of Hamlet's bitterness, how deeply he had drunk of the ghost's poison. I wiped away those stubborn tears as he turned to me again.

'How now, Ophelia?' Father asked gently. 'You need not tell us what Lord Hamlet said as we heard it all.'

I nodded. You care for me, I thought, but all your care has done is bring me to this, and Prince Hamlet too.

Father turned back to the king. 'My lord, let the prince's queen mother talk to him alone, after the play. If she cannot find out what is the matter, then, yes, send him to England.' He hesitated, then added, 'Or confine him here.'

King Claudius nodded. 'It shall be so. Madness in great ones must not unwatched go.'

Chapter 14

The queen met us as we walked back to the great hall. Her ladies trailed behind her, like elderly sparrows behind a cart of grain.

'Well?' she asked abruptly.

King Claudius shook his head.

'Your Majesty, I am sorry,' I said. 'I tried to … to reassure Prince Hamlet, but …' The courtly words that should flow so easily from my tongue refused to come.

Fortunately, my father had them. 'Your Majesty, your son still grieves — over what, we cannot say, though I think it still of love. Perhaps the play tonight will cheer him.'

'Perhaps.' The queen gave me her hand again, making it clear I was still in her favour. 'Ophelia, we hope you will join our pleasures.'

'I … I thank you, madam. I am so sorry I have offended your royal son … he is so angry …' With all women, I thought. He has passed his anguish about your marriage onto me.

'Then you must abate his anger,' she said firmly. She smiled with calculated charm at her husband and my father. 'For a woman leads in love, if not in state. Is that not true, my lords?'

King Claudius smiled. He lifted her hand and kissed it. 'Most true, most wise, most beautiful of women.'

His reply was too pat. What were the king and queen truly thinking under their charm? I wondered. How much love was there, and how much statecraft? I had learned more doubt in the past few months than in all my years of Father's tuition and the library's books.

'The petitioners are waiting, Your Majesty,' murmured Lady Annika, waking from her standing doze.

'Of course.' The queen seemed to have forgotten the crowd waiting in the throne room.

She is worried, I thought, and not just because of Hamlet's possible rebellion. For the first time I saw that she loved him as her son, the child she had carried and cradled, not just as her heir.

'We shall see you tonight, my child,' she told me, then turned, her arm on the king's.

The courtiers followed them along the corridor, my father with them. I waited till they had left, then slowly walked the corridor too, not to the throne room, but to home.

Waiting for the night to come seemed to take a year. I could not read nor sew nor even eat. I left my bread and herring and baked farm cheese, the kind that is stained green with spring nettle juice, for Gerda to eat, and climbed the stairs again into the attic, as if looking out at the world might help me understand it. I longed for the fresh air of my tower. Perhaps the ghost could give me counsel, where mortal advice had failed. But I could not risk being seen creeping about the palace unchaperoned, especially now.

I opened the shutters. I could smell fish being unloaded on the quay. A carter in the courtyard yelled at some boys to get out of the way as his oxen pulled their load of new-cut summer hay. An alewife shouted a greeting to a friend. Beyond the palace gates, the cows had vanished to their summer pasture. A few sheep, newly shorn, blazed fresh white against the summer grass. Geese stepped neatly in a line, herded by a barefoot girl, her hair wrapped in a bright scarf.

A good summer, I thought automatically. I was my father's daughter, after all. No late blizzards to freeze the calves; no storms to sink the fishing boats. Blue skies, no mist to rot the rye. Another winter rich in cheeses and pickled herring, good bread and ale.

If only I could keep an alehouse. Brew barrels, serve customers. Our house was too small a kingdom.

Poor kingdom, I thought, looking out at it. Prosperous now, but did its people suspect the blight ahead? Denmark's harvest was a single prince, and he was mad.

I chewed on my finger. Who could inherit the throne if not Hamlet? I doubted the king or queen would make young Fortinbras their heir. That would be admitting that neither brother had the right to rule. But there was no cousin or nephew of their name; and Denmark's chief lord was my own father. I could not see Father as king; nor the lord of the exchequer, and his only son had died of the flux.

My brother? Laertes could look like a king, but if he had a taste for politics he would be here, at court, where Father could train him to be chancellor in his turn, not playing with the skirts of Paris.

Could Hamlet still become king if he recovered? King Claudius must think so or he'd not send him to England as a cure. Or maybe he hoped that Hamlet might recover enough to marry and have a son, a sensible child who might become king instead. Was that what the queen hoped too? Was Hamlet being sent to England to wed an English princess? I had forgotten how many there were, but England always had them — sisters and daughters and aunts of kings. The English court would not know of his madness, not if he recovered on the voyage.

Perhaps the king was wiser than I'd given him credit for. Elsinore and all its dealings had sent Hamlet mad. If Hamlet were away, no longer angered by the sight of his mother and his uncle, my father and — I bit my finger again — me, he might smile again, grow calm. Be happy. I wanted him to be happy. Even the thought of him married to an English princess didn't hurt me. Much.

It was time to dress. My clothes must fit my state tonight. That would take time.

* * *

Silk petticoat, in pale blue. Brocade overdress ... I shook my head as Gerda brought out the red one. Red was a harlot's colour. Hamlet's words this afternoon still stung. We settled on darker blue, trimmed with silver lace. My mother's pearls at my throat.

I hesitated, my fingers on the locket. I had fastened it about my throat again when Hamlet hadn't taken it, for fear I would drop it. It seemed wrong now to take it off. *Doubt truth to be a liar* ... I kept it on.

Pearl earrings, silk slippers embroidered with pearls, my hair in a silver net touched with pearls too. My clothes would say to the court: the Lady Ophelia has nothing to be ashamed of. Look at her — modesty and wealth combined.

I called the footmen to sweep in front of me so my slippers or hem didn't get dirty as I walked across the courtyard to the palace doors.

'Are you ready, daughter?' Father looked as fine as I, in a gold doublet given to him by the late king as a symbol of his service, red hose and blue garters, his blue cap trimmed with mink. He looked me up and down, then offered me his arm. 'I remember your mother looking much as you do now. She had hair like clouds upon a sunset. A man should not boast, of course, about that which he possesses, but as wife and daughter are made by God and by the noble union that is marriage, perhaps ...'

I let him talk, nodding at the right places. Father was happy again and proud of me, and that was all I needed to hear. He had loved my mother, and loved me.

We crossed the courtyard slowly, the footmen sweeping the way in front of us, two more behind carrying our cloaks. The summer sun lingered on the horizon, unwilling to sleep after sleeping so long in winter. I felt the same.

Tonight, at last, I wanted to smile. A night at court again, conversation, a play! It had been more than a year since I had seen a play. I hadn't heard musicians play since the queen's wedding. There would be supper after the play, and music, dancing. This had been my life, before Hamlet returned to muddle it.

Poor Hamlet. I would be kind tonight, but not familiar. I would behave as befitted my father's daughter and the honour of our house. I would encourage him to go to England, perhaps even tell him quietly to seek happiness there, if I had the chance. He would see truth in my eyes again, for I would mean it, even if it would hurt me to see him come back with an English wife. Surely he would recover once free of Elsinore.

The footmen bowed as we entered the hall. Torches lit the walls, turning the great room to summer too. This was obviously where the play would be performed. Already a stage had been set up at the servants' entrance; and thrones for the king and queen, a seat almost as grand for Hamlet next to the queen, stools for the queen's ladies and the king's men, cushions for the court.

A footman bowed to my father, then spoke softly in his ear.

Father beamed. 'The king wishes us to enter with the royal party,' he told me.

I flushed. This was a sign of favour indeed.

We slipped behind the curtains just as the king and queen came towards us. Behind them walked Lady Annika, muffling a yawn; Lady Anna, in puce that did not suit her; and Lady Hilda, with a froth of lace along her sleeves to hide where her maid had let out the seams. Rosencrantz and Guildenstern walked behind them, dressed in orange velvet and mauve brocade tonight, as fine as peacocks in a barnyard. I wondered where Hamlet was, then heard his voice from the hall. He must be speaking to the players, I thought.

The queen nodded to me to walk beside her, just one pace behind, in front of her other ladies. My father took the other place beside the king. Yes, I thought, tonight will show the court that the House of Polonius has no shame attached to it.

The trumpets sounded. Musicians played the royal march. The king and queen stepped forward as the curtains opened. The members of the court were already on their feet.

I waited till the king and queen had sat, then took the furthest stool as was appropriate for the youngest of the queen's ladies. Lady Annika lowered herself with an audible sigh, and closed her eyes. Lady Hilda and Lady Anna sat upright, as bright as elderly sparrows, excited too.

Hamlet came out from behind the stage. He was dressed presentably tonight, in black silk and satin, with a black hat trimmed with gold. Almost, I thought, like a crown.

The king beckoned him. 'How fares our cousin Hamlet?'

You called him your son four months ago, I thought.

Hamlet smiled; an innocent smile, too merry for the evening. He did not bow. 'Excellent!' He waved his hands. 'I eat the air, promise-crammed.' He bent and whispered so loudly half the hall could hear it: 'You cannot feed capons so.'

My skin prickled. The speech felt wrong. It was a clever man playing at being stupid. How mad was Hamlet? His speech this afternoon before he knew he was being watched had been desperate, but not mad. The fury and insanity had come when he realised I had betrayed him with a watcher behind the tapestry.

I suddenly suspected that Hamlet knew exactly what he was doing. Yet his eyes gleamed too bright.

The king's hands tightened on the armrests of the throne. He could do nothing in front of the court, no matter how much Hamlet mocked him. Hamlet knew it.

'I have nothing with this answer,' King Claudius said stiffly. 'These words are not mine.'

'No, nor mine now,' replied Hamlet gaily. He turned to my father. 'My lord, you acted once at the university?'

'That I did, my lord, and I was accounted a good actor.'

'And what did you enact?' Hamlet asked the question as seriously as if my father had been a master player.

Father did not see that he was being played with. 'I did enact Julius Caesar. I was killed in the Capitol. Brutus killed me.'

Hamlet shook his head, his expression as sad as if the tragedy had just happened. 'It was a brute part of him to kill so capital a calf here.'

I tried not to show my anger. These answers were foolish, but not the answers of a fool. They were also cruel. Somehow Hamlet had guessed that Father had been with the king this afternoon, spying on him. But Father did not deserve this; he had given his life for Elsinore. My love cracked a little, like an abandoned egg. What kind of man would taunt a good man like this? Had Hamlet as much talent for cruelty as his father? I had known the lonely, deserted prince, the lover. What else was he?

'Are the players ready?' Hamlet leaped onto the stage, as bright as any star.

Doubt thou the stars are fire ... I blinked away tears I hadn't felt gathering in my eyes. Did I cry because I had lost Hamlet's love, or because I was losing mine for him? I did not know.

'Yes, my lord.' Rosencrantz gave another of his bows. 'The players stay upon your patience.'

'Come hither, my dear Hamlet. Sit by me,' called the queen.

Hamlet peered at her from the stage as if she were an egg-seller in the market. 'No, good mother,' he said lightly. 'Here's metal more attractive.' Before I realised what was happening, he had jumped down beside me. 'Lady, shall I lie in your lap?'

He sat at my feet, like a child, before I could reply. I flushed. I had never heard a man speak so crudely. Did he mean to humiliate me in front of the entire court? Was this revenge for helping the king and my father spy on him?

'No, my lord,' I said clearly.

He smiled at me, too innocent again. 'I mean, my head upon your lap?'

'Ay, my lord,' I said uncertainly.

I glanced at the queen, but she gave me no hint of what to do. The court stared at us. Even Lady Annika looked at me through half-opened eyes.

'Do you think I meant country matters?' Hamlet's voice was far too loud.

'I think nothing, my lord,' I said carefully.

'That's a fair thought to lie between maids' legs.'

My blush could have heated the castle. 'What is, my lord?' I said, trying to make it seem I had not understood.

'Nothing.'

Hamlet had as good as said that I had lain with him, that I would do so again. Was I supposed to pretend that I hadn't just been insulted in front of everyone who mattered in the kingdom?

'You are merry, my lord,' I said coldly, making sure my voice carried too.

'Who, I?' He blinked up at me, all innocence again.

'Ay, my lord.'

He leaned his head against my legs. I did not dare move away.

'What should a man do but be merry?' He spoke more quietly now. 'Look how cheerfully my mother looks, and my father died within these two hours.'

I kept my hands neatly in my lap, as far from his head as I could. 'Nay, it is twice two months, my lord.'

'So long? Two months ago, and not forgotten yet? Then there's hope a great man's memory may outlive his life by half a year. But, by our lady, he must build churches then; or else he shall be forgotten, like the hobby-horse whose epitaph is "For oh, for oh, the hobby-horse is forgot!"'

I got my breath under control, and my blushes. I even felt a kind of sad relief. The more Hamlet said tonight, the madder he sounded. Everyone who watched us could see it. No one would put any weight on what a madman said to me. I must play the lady-in-waiting, kind and tolerant to her mistress's mad son. I could do that. I could.

But the words from his letter still whispered in my mind. *Doubt truth to be a liar; but never doubt I love.*

What was the truth here? Madness, plots, or love? Or all of them?

The sun shone its evening light across the world outside. Here in the hall, shadows circled and twisted. Footmen brought torches to light the stage.

The play was about to begin.

Chapter 15

The curtain at the servants' entrance parted. Two actors came out, dressed as king and queen. The player queen had not shaved today; I could see the pale fuzz of her young man's beard. She wore a dress that Queen Gertrude had discarded the year before because the moths had eaten holes in each sleeve. They must have been darned for the play, I thought.

The player king and queen embraced on stage. I looked at the real king and queen: they sat politely smiling, thinking it a compliment to them.

The stage queen laid out a blanket, painted as grass and flowers. The stage king lay down, as if asleep. The stage queen left, and another player came through the curtain. He raised his eyebrows at us and held his finger to his lips. He tiptoed up to the sleeping king. I caught my breath.

The actor took off the player king's crown. He kissed it, then put it back. Slowly, looking right and left, he took a vial from his jacket. He held it up for all to see, then bent towards the sleeping king. Slowly, so slowly, the villain poured the poison in the king's ear.

I forced my face to appear calm. I glanced down at Hamlet. He watched King Claudius. His eyes were steady sapphires now, not the wide bright eyes of madness.

King Claudius clutched the arms of his chair. His eyes were stone. His mouth still smiled politely.

Up on the stage, the player queen returned. She kneeled beside the king. She kissed him, then fell back in shock. She clutched her heart, then clasped her hands, imploring to all of us. She kissed the king again and again, lifted his head, then showed us how it lolled. The player king was dead.

I heard a gasp. From Queen Gertrude? But when I glanced up, her face was like a rock.

I stared back at the players. The poisoner slipped back on stage. He lifted the queen's hands and kissed her cheek, as the player king's body was borne from the stage. The player queen shook her head once, twice. But on the third kiss, she smiled and gave the poisoner her lips.

No one in the entire hall moved, except the figures on stage. No one even coughed. How could anyone here miss what this play meant? The wild story Hamlet had told me, which he claimed his father's ghost had told him, had been acted in front of the whole court. Hamlet was mad! He must be mad.

I looked at his face. He did not look mad. For the first time since I had seen him in the glade in the forest, he looked quiet, in control.

I glanced at King Claudius. His face was harder than the palace walls. He saw me looking. I dropped my eyes and hoped my face had not betrayed me.

The players left the stage. The main play, with words, was yet to come; this was only the mime.

I whispered to Hamlet, 'What means this, my lord?'

Hamlet looked at King Claudius still, not at me. 'It means mischief.' His voice was quiet; not that of a madman, nor of one who hated me.

'Will the players give the same tale?' I whispered as the prologue entered, dressed in black velvet.

'We shall know by this fellow.' Hamlet still spoke softly, for me alone to hear. 'The players cannot keep a secret; they'll tell all.'

'Will he tell us what this show meant?'

He looked at me fully then and gave his mad grin. 'Ay, or any show that you'll show him.' He added loudly, 'Be not you ashamed to show, he'll not shame to tell you what it means.'

I tried not to look at those who stared at us.

'You are naught,' I said quietly, but clearly enough for those on either side of us to hear. 'You are naught! I'll mark the play.'

The prologue bowed. 'For us, and for our tragedy,' he proclaimed, 'here stooping to your clemency, we beg your hearing patiently.' And he left the stage, stepping behind the curtain.

'Is this a prologue, or the posy of a ring?' asked Hamlet, again too loudly.

'It is brief, my lord,' I agreed.

He looked up at me. 'As woman's love.'

I shook my head numbly. His look gentled a little.

The player king and queen entered again, and Hamlet turned to them.

The player king began to speak, telling us how he and the queen had been married thirty years.

The player queen clasped her hands and responded. 'So many journeys may the sun and moon make us again count over before our love is done! But woe is me, you are so sick of late. Where love is great, the littlest doubts are fear; where little fears are great, great love grows there.'

The player king kissed the queen's now smooth cheek. Someone had shaved off her beard fluff in the interval. 'Faith, I must leave thee, love, and shortly too, and thou shalt live in this fair world behind, honoured, beloved, and haply one as kind for husband shalt thou —'

'Oh, confound the rest!' the player queen cried. 'Such love must be treason in my breast! In second husband let me be accursed! None shall wed me second, but who killed the first.'

Who killed the first. It was out: the words spoken so everyone in court could hear, but said by an actor, not a prince.

I welded a smile of mild amusement to my face and looked down at Hamlet. His eyes were on the king. 'Wormwood,' he muttered.

Bitter indeed, I thought.

The players were still talking. I hardly heard them. I tried to watch King Claudius and Queen Gertrude without them noticing.

Up on stage, the player king doubted his queen's word. She swore her love, crying that she could never marry again. 'Both here and hence, pursue me lasting strife if once a widow ever I be a wife!'

Hamlet twisted his head to look up into my face. 'If she should break it now,' he said softly.

'Sweet, leave me here awhile,' said the player king. 'I would like to entice the tedious day with sleep.'

The player queen kissed him on the lips. Someone tittered at the back of the hall.

Don't they see what this play is about? I thought. Do they only see a man kissing a young man in a dress?

The player queen left the stage, leaving the player king sleeping on the green and flowery blanket.

'Madam, how do you like this play?' Hamlet called to his mother, his head still resting against my legs.

Queen Gertrude gave a wry smile. 'The lady protests too much, methinks.'

'Oh, but she'll keep her word,' Hamlet said lightly as he turned his head away.

The queen's face showed no guilt, though her eyes were sad. She thinks the poisoning plot is preposterous, I thought. But the play must bring back memories she would rather forget.

But the king? King Claudius bent towards Hamlet, his

voice harsh. 'Do you know the rest of the play? Is there offence in it?'

Hamlet gave his smile of mad innocence. 'No, no, they do but jest, poison in jest. No offence in the world.'

The king stared at him, his face colder than the tower in winter. 'What do you call this play?'

'*The Mouse-trap*,' said Hamlet gaily to the ceiling. 'It is about a murder done in far Vienna. A knavish bit of work, but what of that? Your Majesty, and all of us that have free souls, are not touched by it.'

King Claudius sat back, his face steel.

Hamlet spoke louder still, his voice again the madman's gay lilt. 'Let the sore old horse wince,' he told the ceiling. 'Our withers are not chafed.'

Another actor entered.

'This is one Lucianus, nephew to the king,' said Hamlet, turning his face to me.

I wished he would be quiet. I wished I had never come.

'You are as good as a chorus, my lord,' I said, trying to make it sound as if he was talking about the play.

He moved his head from my legs to look up into my eyes. 'I could even tell you the story of you and your love, if we made it into a puppet show.'

I looked away. 'You are sharp, my lord.'

Please, please, I thought, let them think we are only talking about the play.

'You could blunt my edge, but it might make you moan a little,' said Hamlet softly.

Both better and worse. At least only Lady Anna had heard his crudeness this time. I hoped.

'For better and worse? So must you take your husbands,' said Hamlet. I hadn't realised I'd whispered the words aloud. He sat straighter and called to the players. 'Begin, murderer. Damn you, stop fiddling with your make-up and begin! Come — *the croaking raven doth bellow for revenge.*'

The actor playing Lucianus glanced down at him. I doubted he was used to the audience giving directions. But he began his speech well.

'Thoughts black, hands apt, drugs fit, and time agreeing,' he proclaimed. He looked sneakily to either side, then whispered loudly, 'Confederate season, else no creature seeing.'

He held up the poison. 'Thou mixture rank, of midnight weeds collected, with Hecate's ban thrice blasted, thrice infected.' He kneeled beside the sleeping king. 'Thy natural magic and dire property on wholesome life steal away this healthy life immediately,' he muttered, and lifted the vial and poured the poison in the player king's ear.

The player king gave a small sad grunt. His hands fell back upon the stage.

'He poisons the king in his garden for his kingdom,' said Hamlet conversationally. 'His name is Gonzago. The original story was written in very choice Italian.' He smiled, that innocent smile. 'You shall see how the murderer wins the love of Gonzago's wife,' he added, gazing slowly around the assembled court.

King Claudius gave a grunt of fury. Queen Gertrude clutched his hand, looking puzzled. Claudius shook it off.

I glanced around the audience. Most had one eye on the king's anger, the other on the play. But this play had no brother marrying his sister-in-law, nor was the poisoner the king's brother. Only those who knew or suspected that King Claudius had poisoned his brother would see its mirror in this. Hamlet. The king. And me.

If the king reacted, then we — and the whole court — might see his guilt.

So Hamlet wanted proof of the ghost's words. Not a fool then, nor, I thought, as foolish as he had lately seemed. I thought again of his letter to me: what had he been telling me? *Doubt truth to be a liar …*

On stage, the poisoner gazed in triumph at the body of the player king. King Claudius surged up from his throne.

'The king rises,' I whispered in warning.

Hamlet smiled at me. A real smile. 'What, frightened by false fire?' His voice was equally quiet.

No, I thought, not false fire. I gazed at Hamlet. He nodded. He had done it: proved the ghost's impossible tale to be true.

It was brilliant. It was foolish. It was desperately dangerous, for us all.

The king stood there, in front of all the court. I thought for a second that he might control himself and sit back down.

'How fares my lord?' cried the queen.

Her face was innocent. The king's was not.

'Give me light!' he shouted.

Two footmen grabbed the torches lighting the play and ran towards him. He strode away. The flames cast flickering shadows in the darkness of the corridor.

The lights vanished. The king had fled.

It was impossible. Melodrama. But it was true. King Claudius had killed his brother, Hamlet's father. Poured poison in his ear. No one had witnessed it but the king himself. And now Claudius had shown us that he was guilty.

Chapter 16

The court sat in the shadowed hall, stunned. Even Queen Gertrude sat motionless. The actor who had played the poisoner stood with his mouth open, waiting for a cue, from Hamlet or the other players. It was as if the clocks had stopped in Denmark.

Someone moved. My father. 'Stop the play,' he commanded.

The player nodded gratefully. He slipped behind the curtain. More footmen hurried in, holding flaming torches. Light had reached our world again.

I looked around. Some faces were puzzled. Others were carefully blank. They were the ones who understood. Lady Annika seemed to doze, despite the tumult, but her hands in her lap were tense. Everyone at court would know the truth soon, I thought, as gossip flowed around the palace. But how many would admit that that gossip might be true? Or act upon it? That was the real question.

Perhaps all along some of the council had thought the king's death ... convenient, but they had accepted

Claudius as king. Would that change now, just because of a play? All the play had done was prove the king's guilt; and show King Claudius that Hamlet knew of it. Tonight's demonstration might be brushed off, but every moment Hamlet stayed in Denmark now was a danger to King Claudius and his throne, and to the very peace of Denmark.

I looked at Hamlet, sitting quietly now next to me. It was impossible to read his expression. All about us courtiers were rising, muttering or far too quiet.

'You must go,' Hamlet said softly.

He was not mad; had never been mad. Or only with the anguish that treachery had made. No true madman had connived this.

Doubt truth to be a liar ... I had been a fool! *That* was what his letter to me had meant. Suddenly I realised that he had been telling me to ignore everything he did, all that made him seem mad. I was to trust only one thing: that he loved me.

And despite all I had done, or not done, he still did. Even tonight he had been protecting me, manipulating me into showing the court that I was not a light-of-love who welcomed his advances. His coarseness towards me, so loud, so public, so much the ravings of a madman, had given me the chance to show that I was pure. He had given me back my reputation.

'What comes now?' I whispered.

'Guilt. Innocence. Accusations,' he murmured so only I could hear. 'I must be mad again tonight. Mad till I leave for England. Mad, I am safe. Sane, I am an accuser.' He met my eyes. 'I would not have you see me mad again.'

'My lord, I did not mean ... my father would not allow ...'

I wanted to explain, but had no words. I wasn't even sure what I felt for this man who had twisted my father, myself, his mother, into his play of revenge. But I knew one thing.

I reached into my dress and pulled out his locket. 'You are still against my heart, my lord. It has never left me. Never.'

'Then let my heart stay here, safe with you. You must go now.'

'My lord, you will ... you will take care?'

'I will be mad most carefully.' He took my hand and kissed it briefly.

I wanted to ask what he planned to do in England. England was our ally, but would it support Claudius for king, or Hamlet? Claudius was king already. But Hamlet could offer the English king what Claudius could not: a marriage, between Hamlet and England. I sat like a statue, feeling his warmth beside me. No, I did not doubt his love. A prince may love wherever he likes. But his marriage must be for his country.

I found my voice. I even kept it steady. 'My lord, I wish you well in England. In whatever you must choose there.'

I meant the words. They were the hardest gift I had ever given.

He met my eyes. Had he understood?

'I must see my mother now, before I leave,' he said.

This was goodbye. If Hamlet returned wed, I could not be a royal mistress. A miller's daughter might, but not I. Not if I wanted to keep my father's honour. I loved my father. I found, suddenly, that I cared for myself too. I would be no man's, bound by his whim.

I stood, wishing I could stay, wanting to advise him, quietly, as my father had advised his father. Hamlet was not mad. Nor was he a fool. But he had not been wise either.

Playing mad had lulled King Claudius's suspicions for a while, had convinced him that Hamlet wasn't trying to win the lords over to his side in rebellion. But those same lords would be even less likely to support Hamlet now. The lords would always wonder if he had truly been mad, might become mad again. History remembered too many mad kings and the horrors of their times.

If Hamlet had only done what I had asked the first day we met: played the sober dutiful prince, gained the trust of the lords of Denmark. Instead, he had lost even the rags of their regard, and gained nothing, not even me. Only the certainty of King Claudius's guilt. Did knowing his father's ghost had not lied mean so much to him?

I looked at him, standing alone despite the people all around. Always alone, I thought. Always wondering who is his true friend, or who, like Rosencrantz and Guildenstern, love him only because he is a prince. Even I ... I swallowed, the truth bitter in my throat. Even I.

'Go,' said Hamlet softly. 'Do not look at me. I would not have you in danger with me for the world. Go now.'

'My lord,' I whispered, and turned towards the door, my face blank. I heard a murmur, so soft it might have been the wind: *'Doubt that the sun doth move ...'*

I would not cry. I felt Lady Annika's gaze on me, briefly, as she and Lady Anna and Lady Hilda clustered about the queen. I curtseyed to her. For the first time since I had known her, Queen Gertrude looked bewildered. I could not see my father.

All around me people jostled towards the door. I had never heard a crowd so silent. No one wanted to be seen talking tonight, in case someone wondered they whispered treason.

I wanted to turn and watch Prince Hamlet go. I wanted to feel his kiss, once more. Just once. Wanted to comfort him. Most of all I wanted to try to steady him, an unchecked raft upon the snow-fed stream of anger and revenge.

But I was just a girl. I let myself be carried out among the throng.

Gerda waited to undress me. I shook my head. 'Get yourself to bed,' I told her.

'But, my lady —'

'Gentle Gerda. Go.'

This night was not finished yet. I glanced outside. The summer sun had finally sunk to its brief rest, but what had been stirred up in the palace could not be calmed. Scrambled eggs cannot be unscrambled. Cheese will not turn back to milk. King Claudius had shown his guilt to Hamlet tonight. Others must be wondering, and watching. King Claudius had killed once to get his throne. Would he kill Hamlet now to keep it?

I had to speak to Father. Should have spoken to him before. Father must know how things truly stood, what Hamlet believed, what King Claudius had shown to be true. Father might seem foolish, but he knew this nation. Suddenly I wondered if Father put on his cloak of pomposity to hide his wisdom, as Hamlet had used madness. The most powerful lord in Denmark might be a threat to a king. But Father had carefully never challenged anyone.

I strode up and down the room, unable to settle. What was Hamlet doing? He had said he must see his mother, but was that all he planned? Would he confront the king before he left for England? Even fight him for the kingdom? Hamlet wore a rapier, like every man of fashion.

No, King Claudius would not let a fight settle who would win the throne of Denmark. He already had the kingdom. He was an old man too; he would not risk a fight, certainly not against a much younger man. He would call his guards and have Hamlet executed; end the risk like a farmer chopping off a goose's head.

Or would he? To openly execute Hamlet now would be admitting his own guilt. Surely Hamlet would have the sense to leave the court for England quickly, as he had planned. To let gossip against the king brew, while he was safely away …

I shook my head to try to clear it. I could not think here, confined inside the house. It was obvious that Father wasn't coming straight home. Whatever was happening at the palace, he was part of it. He might even sleep there, as he did some nights when the parliament sat late.

I made myself wait till all the lights in our house were out. I took a candle and crept to the door to the palace, still in the clothes I had worn to the play. It was a risk, but a slight one. I had never met anyone in my journeys to the tower before. Except, of course, a ghost. With so much happening tonight, I could not risk being found in boy's clothes. I might need to speak to Father, even to attend the queen.

I opened the door and peered down the dim corridor. No one.

I left my candle on the lower steps up to the tower, so it would not blow out, and climbed the rest of the way by starlight. *Doubt thou the stars are fire* … Oh, Hamlet, I thought. My heart felt ripped to linen shreds.

The wind moaned around the battlements. It felt strange to be up here in a dress. The wind tugged at my skirts and I had to hold them down, till I realised that no one could see my legs here, except perhaps an owl.

I sat on the battlements, drawing my skirts around me for warmth. The sea muttered behind me, but I could smell dung heaps and green grass. Yes, I could think up here, with the kingdom stretched before me.

Hamlet was not mad. He was playing at madness; like the actors played, in a play he had arranged. His wild story was true. King Claudius was guilty. But who else? The queen? No. I knew her too well. She had looked puzzled, not stricken.

My father? A definite no to that too. Father could never imagine murdering a king. Or that his daughter might dress up as a man to have her freedom for a few hours each night.

I felt the wind pull and twist at my petticoats, while slapping the waves against the castle walls. The graveyard and royal garden lay dark below me, but I could almost see the far-off forest in the starlight. A thousand blue-black greens touched with gold and silver, winking at the stars until the forest met the sky. On the other side, I could just make out the farms with their earth formed neatly into rectangles, the fields of beet and barley and rye clothing the world, the black splodges of pigsties and dung piles.

Most ladies of the court held clove-studded oranges to their noses when their litters were carried past a farmer's pigsty. But I enjoyed the smell. Pigsties meant sausages and hams; they meant red-cheeked children, not starving waifs. Dung heaps stank, but when the dung was spread out on the fields, it made them green.

Dung heaps were ... sensible. Like cheese. Pretending to be mad wasn't sensible. Denmark's lords would never accept a madman as their king. Hamlet was a scholar; surely he must know that. But he had pretended madness. Why?

And suddenly I saw it all, as if daylight speared down onto my tower.

From the moment he heard that his father had been murdered, Hamlet had known that the king planned to kill him too.

My advice to make alliances with the lords of court had been most sensible. But it would have killed him. A sensible young prince, the true heir to the throne — especially one married to the lord chancellor's daughter — would be a threat. One day, King Claudius would offend this lord or that, and they would say, 'The king dodders. And, after all, he is no true king. He is but a steward for Prince Hamlet.'

Hamlet had to pretend to be mad with me as well. Anything I repeated to my father or the queen about ghosts and poison in the king's ear would be dismissed as a madman's ravings.

I clutched at my skirts again as the wind tried to carry them away. Claudius had killed once — not a man in battle, not even an enemy, but his own brother and his king. A man who had killed his king and brother would kill his nephew with no more concern than if he slapped a gnat. Hamlet's pretended madness had saved his life.

King Claudius would kill me too, if he suspected I was plotting with Hamlet; or even if he simply thought he would be safer with me gone.

I looked out at the darkness. Where was old King Fortinbras when I needed his advice? But he would not help me now. King Fortinbras might forswear vengeance, but I didn't think he would help the son of his enemy.

What could I do? What could any girl do? Only kings and queens had power.

The wind was sweet, the breath of flowers. Below me in the palace, I heard curses, shouting, a woman's scream. A servant had dropped a tray, I thought. Broken china, food on the floor. A broken kingdom would be ripe for civil war, or for invasion. Could it be pieced together again?

I breathed in the scents of grass and ripening cheeses. Men made war. Women made cheese, tended boys who cut their knees, nursed wounded warriors. Perhaps women could mend cracked kingdoms too.

I must go to the queen. She would be cleft in twain tonight, seeing her husband's guilt, learning the role she had been fooled to play. She loved her son, and her husband. Perhaps she even loved me too, a little. But she loved another more than any of us. The kingdom. If anyone could untangle the threads of Denmark's future, it would be the queen.

I must ask for a private audience with her; no old ladies nodding over their embroidery. Hamlet would not give up his vengeance, nor the king give up his throne. I could see only three possible futures: Hamlet would kill Claudius, or Claudius would kill Hamlet; or both would raise an army and lead the whole kingdom into civil war. It must not happen! The queen and I could prevent it. She could speak to the king, and I to Hamlet.

Men enjoyed hearing the trumpets calling them to war, fighting with rapiers and spearing deer with lances. Women know the important things: children, cheese, fat pigs and love.

Suddenly I could see a fourth way. A sensible solution, bringing peace, not clashing swords. Hamlet must go to England, let the talk die down. King Claudius could enjoy some years in the sun. When Hamlet returned in two years, or three, the court's memory of his madness would be forgotten. King Claudius would abdicate. There would be no accusations of murder; just an organised handover of crown and power. No vengeance, nor justice either. Peace and prosperity instead. Cheese does not care about justice, as long as it is drained and turned. A kingdom too needed care more than justice for its prince and king.

Queen Gertrude would understand that. And Claudius could not rule without her favour, if she gave it to her son.

The wind gusted around me, cold and strong, as if trying to blow my thoughts away. The stars twinkled like fire-lit tin. Hamlet still loved me. He would listen to me. Even pretending to be mad, he had sat by me, claiming me before the court. And one day — a peaceful day — King Hamlet and Queen Ophelia might sit side by side on their thrones, all the roses of summer around them, while Gertrude sat with her grandchildren around her knee …

A cry split the darkness.

'Murder!'

Chapter 17

The dream shattered. I gathered my skirts and sprinted down the tower steps. The candle flickered and went out. I smoothed my hair and ran along the privy corridor, then out into a larger one, well-lit.

I grabbed a serving woman's arm. 'What's happened?'

The servant pulled away from me and swept her apron over her face. 'Oh, woe! Woe! Alack, for he is dead!'

'Who is dead? Answer me!'

Hamlet, I thought. King Claudius has murdered Hamlet. Killed my dreams, my future, my love …

'Lady Ophelia!' It was Lady Annika's maid, a quiet woman, sensible. She curtseyed deeply. 'Her Majesty would speak with you.'

'Of course,' I said automatically. 'Please, who is dead?'

She looked uncomfortable. 'It is that which the queen wishes to speak to you about, my lady.'

'Is it Prince Hamlet?' I whispered.

The maid shook her head, obviously surprised at the suggestion. 'No, my lady.'

'The king?' How would the lords react if Hamlet had killed the king? Would they support him? Or execute him?

'Not His Majesty either, my lady.'

I felt my heart unclench a little.

'If your ladyship will come?'

I swept along the corridor, hoping my hair was not too out of order. Where there were men and swords and spirits, there would be murder. Some guard with a hip flask had stabbed another. The queen wished her ladies to stay with her while she bade the servants to go about their work, the court to go to bed.

I almost believed it.

I waited while the maid opened the door to the queen's apartments. 'My Lady Ophelia,' she announced. I sank into a curtsey, glad I still wore my finery.

'Dear child.' The queen came towards me from the cluster of her maids and ladies, and took my hand to raise me up. Her own hands were cold. 'Sit by the fire.'

She led me to her own chair. 'Sit,' she repeated. 'Lady Hilda, the posset.'

I took the goblet, felt its warmth on my wind-cold hands. Why did I need a posset?

The maids left suddenly, without instruction, as if the tide had gone out, leaving Lady Annika dozing on a cushion next to the flames, and Lady Hilda and Lady Anna looking at me with expressions I could not read. Did not want to read …

'I have news for you.' The queen took my hand again. 'Ill news, which cannot be kept in a closet till we are ready. Ophelia, your gentle father has been killed.'

'Father?' I stared at her. Other men died in violence, but not Father. Father was dry and sober, with his accounts and his advice. Men like my father died as old bones in their beds. 'How? Why?'

'An accident. It was an accident.' The queen's voice trembled slightly.

I sensed Lady Annika glance at us, but when I looked over at her, her eyes were shut.

'What accident?' Had Father fallen down the stairs? But Father was cautious; he never drank too much, always held the balustrade as he descended the staircase.

The queen hadn't cried when the old king died. I had never seen her cry. But her face was wet now. 'It was my son. My poor, mad son, our Hamlet. He thought he heard a rat behind the tapestry. He stabbed it with his sword.' Queen Gertrude shut her eyes briefly, as if in pain, then added, 'But it was your father.'

Father? Gone? My first thought was of cheese. Goat's cheeses, made from milk simmered till it was as yellow as honey, then drained. We had two score in the cellar, because Father loved them. No one else in the household could stand the smell. Who would eat his cheeses now? Who would wear the cuffs I embroidered for him, almost complete?

Only then did I think: Father has left me too. Father was the rock that sheltered me; a rock I had dodged around sometimes, never valuing him enough till he was gone. Gone. My brain could not take it in. All my life had been measured in Father's breakfasts, dinners, mending his linen, hearing his talk about the world of Denmark and beyond.

Father had so many words. And now just one. Gone.

I looked at the queen's hands with their age spots, at my hands, unwrinkled. Questions seeped into my brain. Why had Hamlet used a rapier on a rat? He'd had larger game to hunt tonight. A madman might have done it. But Hamlet was not mad. Was he?

And what was my father doing behind a tapestry in the queen's bedroom? Spying on her? Impossible. Spying on Hamlet again? That fitted. But Hamlet could never have mistaken a man's shape for a rat; my father's least of all. If Hamlet had thrust his rapier into someone through the tapestry hanging on the wall, he had meant to do it. But there was only one person Hamlet wanted to kill; the man he had glimpsed behind the tapestry in the library.

Hamlet had tried to kill the king.

No accident then, no matter what Queen Gertrude told me now. 'Murder!' they'd called; not 'The lord chancellor has been killed by mistake.' The court believed Hamlet had murdered my father. It *had* been murder, even if the wrong man had died.

I kept my voice steady. 'Where is Prince Hamlet now?'

'Gone to England.'

'What? Already?'

I felt cold, as if the fire had vanished. Grief for my father shot through me again like ice-melt down the river. Gone. And Hamlet gone too. My brother far away …

Suddenly a maid was there with a cushioned chair. Queen Gertrude sank into it, next to me. 'It was an accident,' she repeated. 'I saw it and can testify that it was so. But others might think … It was best to get Hamlet away, my dear, till talk dies down. The voyage may soothe his mind too.'

'He … he left willingly?'

'Yes, dear child.'

There was something in her voice. She spoke the truth, but not all the truth. What was she keeping from me?

'No word to me?' I whispered.

'My dear, his mind is too disordered. When he is himself again, I am sure he will turn to you. He will love us both again …' Her voice died away.

What of me now? I did not say the words aloud, but the queen answered them.

'The king has already sent word to your brother. You must think of us as your parents, until your brother comes.'

My brother, dear Laertes. He would be head of our house now, lord of our estates. He would direct my life with love and kindness. I shut my eyes in gratitude that I had such a brother, one who had no part in any palace plots.

'My dear?'

I opened my eyes at the queen's concern. Did she think I had fainted? I tried to keep my voice steady. 'Where is Father's body, madam?'

'It lies in state, within the chapel. Lady Anna will take you there soon.' She glanced at Lady Anna, who nodded sympathetically.

The servants will be tidying away all signs of murder, I thought. Changing his clothes, washing off the blood. Neither I nor the court would see my father till he was the lord chancellor again, not a man just slain.

The door opened. King Claudius strode in.

I rose and curtseyed, trying to keep the dreadful knowledge from my face. This man had killed his brother; and, somehow, that had led to my father's death as well.

'Rise, my child.' The king looked at his wife. 'Have you told her?'

'I have told her the truth, my lord. That her father was killed by accident. That Prince Hamlet is gone to England. The sea air on the voyage will help him to recover.'

'Yes. It was an accident.' The king looked at me, his eyes as blank as the inside of a cooking pot.

He is wondering what Hamlet has told me, I thought. He saw my face when the player king was poisoned on stage. He must be wondering what I will tell the court now. What I might tell my brother.

I had to leave. Get away from court. Put plots and poisonings behind me. I could do no good here now. If I stayed, Claudius might have me killed.

'I thank Your Majesty for your kindness,' I said carefully. 'I beg your permission to return to our estates in the country to wait there for my brother. I ... I would like the quiet, to grieve for my father.'

'No, no!' King Claudius smiled, but those cold eyes stayed watchful. 'We cannot have you so far from our care, not orphaned as you are. You are ours now, to cherish.'

I said nothing. What is there to say when a king and queen give an order? I curtseyed again, and let Lady Anna and Lady Hilda lead me from the room.

I slept at last, an hour perhaps. I woke as the sun turned the sky grey. The servants were not up. They too, perhaps, had wept late last night. Our house was masterless till Laertes returned. The servants would expect me to sleep late too, but I could not stay in our house, weeping privately as a daughter should. With every glance I expected to see my father there: a gravy stain on his doublet for me to wipe off, calling for extra candles to aid his failing eyesight as he peered at the accounts ... Gone. Both of them gone, my father and my lover.

Sane or mad, Hamlet was beyond my reach. My brother might be weeks away. And I was at the king's mercy. I couldn't go to our estates, not against his order. Nor did I dare go up to my tower in daylight.

But there was somewhere I could go. Somewhere with peace, and beauty. Somewhere that never changed.

I dressed in a simple shift and took my green cloth cloak. Under its hood I might be a lady or a lady's maid, or even a tavern-keeper's wife. I slipped out the servants' door, then across the drawbridge.

It was market day in the square. Gentlefolk might sleep until the sun bounced above the horizon, but not farmers and carters. They had been up for hours in the pre-dawn light. The flocks of sheep, the goats and pigs must have been sold earlier so the new owners could get them home by dark. Even the barrels of fish were emptying as other households' servants bought the week's provisions.

I slipped between stalls of red cabbages and vats of spiced herring. A butter-seller held up her wares, a reindeer stamped on each round yellow pat. 'Sweet butter! New butter!' Last week I would have stopped to buy some — my father loved fresh butter that tasted of sunlight and green grass after a long winter of eating butter salted and fermented.

My father. I blinked the tears away.

I pushed my way through the crowd, then turned at the gates, towards the king's forest rather than the road. The glade where Hamlet had kissed me would still be there, quiet, unseen by anyone.

'*Doubt that the sun doth move,*' I whispered. That was all I had now — words. Memories. And a brother, I told myself. A good brother, who will protect you. Find you a husband ... My body shivered, despite my cloak and the sun. When I last pushed under these branches, I had thought I had everything I'd ever dreamed of. A lover, a family, a future where I would be queen. Now …

I ducked under the last big branch. There it was — the glade. The ice had melted. The stream was a river now, running fast with melted snow. A few late spring flowers still dotted the grass — anemones and bluebells. I will pick a bunch for Father's desk, I thought. And remembered.

'Ophelia.'

I turned. He stood beneath the pine tree in a travelling cloak like mine, though his was black. Black for mourning, I thought. I must put on black now too.

'I … I thought you had left for England last night,' I said stupidly.

I waited for my heart to beat drum-like on seeing him. Waited for my skin to yearn for his. But I felt empty, and as alone as he was.

'Even my uncle cannot order a ship to set off at night, without a moon to guide her. We sail with the next tide.' Hamlet added simply, 'I'm sorry. I didn't mean to kill him.'

He didn't step closer. I did not go to him.

'You thought my poor father a rat?'

'I thought your poor father the king, scuttling rat-like behind my mother's tapestries. Ophelia, I am not mad. I put on the robe of madness to hide my purpose from my uncle, till I could see if what my father's ghost claimed was truth.'

He stepped towards me then, but I stepped back, beyond his reach.

'You tried to kill a king, yet you did kill my father.'

'I thought I had killed my father's murderer! I had been … arguing with my mother.' Hamlet's face twisted. 'If it is arguing to tell your mother she is a whore, who married the man who killed her husband to satisfy the lustful pleadings of her aged flesh.' He shut his eyes, last night's pain a slash across his face. 'I did my father's bidding!' he whispered. 'My father's ghost appeared there in my mother's chamber, urging revenge. So I unsheathed my rapier and stabbed!' His voice rose, pleading, desperate. 'What else must a son do when his father's ghost cries for his killer's blood?'

He glanced back towards Elsinore. I could see the effort he made to calm himself. 'Perhaps I was mad,' he whispered, 'when my father's ghost urged me on. Would you forgive me if it were true madness that brought me to slay your father?'

Forgive him? I did not know. But I remembered the wisdom of another ghost. Do not cling to anger and revenge, King Fortinbras had told me. For if I did, I would become what Hamlet was now, less of a man, because the greater part was bitterness and hatred.

I said, 'I know only this, my lord, that I am yours.'

His face relaxed. He hears only what he wants to hear, I thought. He does not hear that I have not forgiven him; nor that I have not said the words 'I love you still'. But when he took my hand, I did not draw away.

He said abruptly, 'My uncle plans to have me killed in England.'

I stared. Of all things, I had not imagined that. 'What? How do you know?'

'He gave me a letter to take to the king of England, asking him to execute the bearer.' His smile darkened in contempt. 'Did he think a prince of Denmark would hesitate to break the king's seal? I am the true king of Denmark, not he! My kind uncle cannot execute me here at Elsinore. My mother has made herself believe he is innocent of one murder, but even she will not let him kill me.'

He said it so flatly that I knew there was no madness in him now.

'What did you do with the letter?' I asked.

He gave the warped smile again. 'I sealed it anew. My uncle forgets that I have a royal seal, much like the one he uses now. I warrant the king of England will see no difference.'

'What will you do?' I whispered.

'Sail to England, as I am supposed to do. But my so-called friends, who do my uncle's bidding, shall give the king the letter. Let them lose their lives. I will tell the English king all that has happened, and return with an English army. If young Fortinbras can lead an army, so can I.'

Could he? Even if he could, was that what our country needed — a foreign army to give us a king? Brother killing brother, crops burned or never sown?

He bent and kissed me. This time his lips were cold.

'I must go, before they find me. Go to your estates,' he said quickly. 'Stay safe and wait for me.'

He kissed me again, hard and long. I don't think he realised that my lips did not move under his, nor my body press to his.

At last he stepped back. He stroked my cheek. 'Fair Ophelia, how I love thee. Guard yourself, for you belong to me.'

He turned, and almost ran back through the trees.

I touched my cheek where his glove had stroked me. My father's murderer had kissed me. Yesterday I had thought him mad. Today? I did not know. Could a madman have planned that play that made the king cry out in guilt? Pretending madness may have saved his life too. Yet last night I had seen Hamlet swing from sorrow to wild glee, capering and jumping about the stage. That had not been pretence; nor were the words spoken to himself in the library, as he wondered if he should live with all his burdens or free himself and die.

No, not mad. But not entirely sane.

I was lucky with my ghost, I thought. My ghost had loved his son. He did not shriek and seek revenge. If Hamlet was mad, his father had led him to it.

I sat on a lichen-covered log and gazed at the river. Had Hamlet never wondered why the court and people had accepted his uncle, had shown so little grief when their former king was dead? Old King Hamlet was the man who had cheated the rightful king of his throne. A man his wife had loved so little she had married within weeks of his death, and not just to keep the country stable. Claudius and his brother were like two raw peas in a pod, both cruel and hard.

And Hamlet? I had told him I belonged to him. I did not lie, but I belonged to him only because I belonged to no one else now. My father was dead, my brother was far away, the queen I had almost loved had been taken in by a murderer. I was Hamlet's or I was no one's. And he was prince of Denmark, mad or sane. I was enough my father's daughter to know that mattered.

The breeze freshened through the leaves, sending them shivering. I could smell cold water, new grass, and hear the far-off tinkle of bells as the cows wandered to pasture after their morning milking. Some farm girl would be making cheese.

The thought steadied me. Kings came and went, and so did passion. But cheese continued for as long as women had the sense to milk the cows, drain the whey, and store the cheeses properly. Women like me. I had no father to belong to now; but I had myself.

'I belong to me,' I whispered.

It was as if a sack of rocks had fallen from my back. I heard the flicker of swallows as they snapped at gnats above me, heard the song of leaves and trees, all that I had missed in my sorrow. Suddenly I could think clearly again.

I picked a jonquil, breathed in its scent, then sat on the log again, drawing my cloak around me. Would the English king give Hamlet an army? Perhaps. But only if Denmark became a vassal state of England, our king forever owing his throne to a foreign power.

If the king of England granted Hamlet an army, King Claudius would hear of it. And he would not hesitate to get rid of a girl who might persuade Queen Gertrude that her son was right and his own actions were wrong. A girl who had seen him start with guilt at the play. A girl known to be sensible, whose word would carry weight. The daughter of the late lord chancellor, the second most important man in all the land, respected, even loved, where neither this king nor his brother had been.

A robin danced among the flowers as I accepted the inevitable. My life was in danger. If I seemed even to breathe out of turn, Claudius would kill me too.

I had nowhere to run; no one to ask for help, until my brother came. I didn't even have a sword to defend myself. I must seem meek, glad of Their Majesties' comfort. I must smile and smile.

The thought reminded me of something Hamlet had said: 'A man can smile and smile and still be a villain.' I looked at the flower in my hand. The only weapons a girl had were smiles and blossoms.

Chapter 18

We buried my father three days later, in the graveyard I had watched over so often from the tower. He wore his newly embroidered cuffs, which I had finished the night before.

The king led the procession, and I walked at the queen's side, but neither spoke to me. Behind us came Lady Annika, Lady Anna and Lady Hilda, and a small party of the king's men. The queen's ladies had each kissed me upon the cheek and pressed my hand and whispered words of condolence. I hardly heard them. How could old women's sympathy help me now?

A small procession seemed a poor farewell for the man who had given so much to Denmark.

It is the custom after a funeral for guests to take a cup to toast the family's loss. But the members of the royal party were the only mourners here, and I couldn't invite the king and queen to come to our house. They alone could grant the honour of visiting their subjects. I'd had the servants prepare wine and cakes in case they suggested it, but they didn't. When the funeral words were said, when we had walked the short way from the graveyard to the palace, I received a pat on the cheek from the queen, another kiss from her ladies, and a sentence of warning rather than comfort from the king, though it was lightly said. 'We are glad to see you stay here, Lady Ophelia.'

I sank into a curtsey, my black silk skirts rustling. 'As Your Majesty directs, so do I obey.' By the time I had risen, they had gone.

Gerda waited for me at the palace steps. She followed me back home; helped me change from black silk to black bombazine. It seemed there would be no callers today, nor could I go out for the next three months of mourning. A good daughter hid her face and mourned. It was all I wished to do.

You do not know your loss until you feel it. I had laughed at Father's long-winded speeches, thought little of his wisdom because he so enjoyed dispensing it. Yet it *was* wisdom. And if he had not always acted wisely, who in this kingdom had? Father had done better than most, and with a better heart.

A good epitaph for any man, I thought, as I sat dressed in black, the house's curtains drawn, the doors shut to the summer breeze, as was proper for a house of mourning.

No one came. Not the queen, to tell me of her sorrow. Not Ladies Anna, Annika or Hilda. No visits of condolence. Usually, friends send food to a house of mourning, to feed the family in their grief and the mourners at the funeral. But no haunches of venison were delivered to our kitchen, no hare pies, no flasks of pickled herring or loaves of fresh rye bread.

During those long weeks I learned how truly alone I was.

All my life, the dining table had been spread for each meal with cheeses, breads, ale, meat and fish, dishes of fresh or dried fruits, olives, nuts; the silver salt cellar, the silver butter platters, the silver centrepieces, all well-polished. There seemed little point in all that work just for me. I ate barley bread and cheese, sitting on the cushions in my sewing room. Only the cheeses changed as the weeks went by. Green cheese gave way to Wette Willie; then the small oval cheeses soaked in whey that we call 'cheeses of the Moon'.

Gerda sat with me, mending a petticoat, while I read one of Father's books: the play he had told Hamlet he had acted in all those years before. I almost smiled to think of my portly father as Caesar. Better to smile than cry.

Gerda sliced another hunk of cheese for me: a plain Summer Round today. 'There are strawberries in the market,' she said, trying to tempt me. 'Would you like me to buy you some, my lady?'

I shook my head. I did not want to send Gerda or the footmen out to the market, in case seeing my servants reminded King Claudius of me. All I can do, I thought, is wait for Laertes.

'Laertes! Laertes!' The yells came from outside, as if my imagining had conjured up a crowd to call his name.

'Has Lord Laertes come?' cried Gerda.

I ran to the front window and peered out. There was no sign of my brother's horse or carriage. Instead, a rabble yelled at the palace walls, men waving hoes and picks and rakes. 'Laertes!' they shouted. 'Laertes must be king! We want Laertes!'

The butter-sellers took up the chant. 'We want Laertes! We want Laertes!'

I looked towards the palace. The doors were closed and bolted. Up on the battlements, men in armour held their bows at the ready to speed their arrows down.

I let the curtain fall.

'Why does the crowd call your brother's name?' asked Gerda uncertainly.

'They want him to be king,' I said.

'King!' Gerda almost glowed. 'That would be wonderful.'

'No. It may mean our deaths. It is treason to even say the words! Stop the other servants talking about it too. No one must leave the house. No one! You understand?'

'Yes,' she whispered.

I had been stupid, sitting here in my grief without thinking of what else might be happening in the kingdom. Others had seen the signs of the king's guilt that night, servants as well as lords and ladies. Word had spread. Treason was a dish best served in private. It seemed the men yelling my brother's name had eaten of it too.

175

The people of Denmark didn't want a poisoner for a king, nor his mad nephew Hamlet. They wanted Laertes, son of their good lord chancellor.

Was Laertes behind this? I wondered. Was he planning rebellion? Or did the crowd shout his name because it was the only one they trusted?

I had no way of knowing. But I had to act quickly. My first duty was to keep the servants safe. How long would it be before guards came here; men with swords to take me to the palace? To imprison my servants in case they tried to warn Laertes?

'Gerda, go to the kitchen, if you please. I would like herring pies made. A host of pies for when my brother comes. You must help the cook make them.'

'Me, my lady? I have no hand for pastry.'

'Then you must pick out the fishbones.'

The palace guards were good men, even if they obeyed an evil king. They would recognise the truth if Gerda and the other servants said honestly that they didn't know where I was, and hadn't heard from Laertes either. Servants planning rebellion didn't have time to decorate herring pies.

I ran up to my room. Had Laertes arrived in Denmark already? Had he brought an army — men from our estates and soldiers from the other lords' estates? Or were the people yelling his name simply because they'd had enough of the family who had won the kingdom in a bet, then plotted and murdered each other. My father had been the best of men compared to the two kings he had served. Laertes must seem a paragon compared to Hamlet, who they thought was mad, and a murderer too.

Poor Hamlet. I realised suddenly that any love I still felt for him was like that of a mother for her child. Poor lonely man, kept away from his land and his family so long, unfit and untutored to carry the burdens life had given him.

But I must watch out for myself now. If I had been in danger as Hamlet's love, I was in worse danger as the sister of the man the people wanted as their king. King Claudius could take me hostage and tell my brother, 'Disband your army or we will kill your sister. Come any closer to Elsinore and we will cut off her head and raise it above the battlements as a warning to all traitors.'

I had to flee. But how? This house was watched, so close to the palace. Even if I managed to sneak out, I would be found before I had put any real distance behind me. Perhaps there were watchers along the roads to our estates, to see if I disobeyed the king's orders and tried to escape to safety.

Where could I hide? Under the bed, like a child playing hide and seek? Even if I vanished into my tower, the guards would search every corner of our house and the palace till they found me.

I looked about my room, as if the cushions and rugs might help me. Some flowers I had arranged in vases weeks ago were faded now, their water dried. Suddenly it came to me. I still had a girl's weapons: smiles and flowers. If I used them properly, I might, perhaps, survive.

I chose my dress with care: a linen shift, bleached
by the sun and age. It had been my mother's, and my
grandmother's. Good linen grows softer with the years.
I felt it caress my skin as Gerda dropped it over my
shoulders. I hoped I had their blessing as I wore it. I
needed blessings now.

Gerda fastened on the wide black silk skirt held out
with whalebone. It had been my mother's too, part of the
mourning clothes every family kept.

'No, don't sew it on,' I said quickly. 'Just use a sash.'

She stared. 'But, my lady, what if you trip on your
skirt? It might fall off if it is not sewn on.'

'Peasant girls manage not to lose their skirts,' I said.
'No, do not sew my sleeves on either. Just tie them up
with a ribbon.'

'You cannot wear tied-on sleeves to court!' Gerda
hesitated. 'That is where you're going, isn't it?'

Where else would I wear black silk?

'Yes. Give me a shawl to cover the ribbons. That will
do. Now leave me. Go back to making the pies. I … I
need to think before I leave the house.'

'Yes, my lady,' Gerda said doubtfully.

'Gerda, will you do something else for me?'

'Of course. Anything at all, my lady.' She glanced out
the window to where the rabble still called my brother's
name. 'We all would, my lady,' she said softly. 'Every

servant. Every man on the estates. Whatever you and Lord Laertes need.'

My heart ached at her kindness. I forced myself to smile. 'It won't come to that,' I said, and pressed two gold coins into her hand.

She looked at them, as surprised as if they had been eggs. 'I don't understand, my lady.'

'The queen may wish me to stay at the palace,' I said carefully. 'If I should not return this afternoon, that money and the food in the cellar will keep the household till my brother returns.' And for months afterwards if he rebels, I thought.

Gerda looked at me. She was no fool. 'Madam, you know I would give my life for you.'

'But I want you to keep it.' I kissed her cheek. 'Leave me now.'

I thought she might argue, but after another serious look at me, she bobbed a curtsey, and shut the door behind her as she left the room.

I bent and stripped off the stockings she had put on me. I stuffed one with Laertes's old shirt, the other with the breeches I sometimes wore at night. I added men's shoes. They were bulky, but with a lot of shoving I got them in. I tied the stockings about my waist, under the wide skirt, then jumped up and down to see if they fell off. They didn't.

Now for the flowers, my final weapon. Faded flowers, from the vases. I pulled my hair loose from Gerda's careful plait and poked the flowers in hither and thither, knotting my hair in places to hold them. Dead flowers for a poor mad girl.

Sauce for the gander can be sauce for the goose. If Hamlet could play mad, then I could too.

Chapter 19

I couldn't leave by the front door. Not like this. Some kind soul in the marketplace would bring me back. A palace guard might be watching the doors to make sure I did not leave the house.

I climbed up to the second floor and looked at the door to the palace. Would it be bolted? Or would there be a guard waiting on the other side?

I took a deep breath. If there was no guard, I would leave aside these dreams of persecution and take up my books again. If there was no guard, I was safe.

I reached forward with one hand and swung the door open.

'My lady?' The guard stared at me, startled. His sword stayed at his side, but it was there, as was he, standing where no guard or sword had been before. 'My Lady Ophelia, I am afraid I have orders not to let you pass.'

I smiled. I picked a dead flower from my hair. I offered it to him.

The guard stared at it. He could have coped with a sword, even a kitchen knife, but he had no idea what to do with a flower.

'Pray take it.' I made my voice light, a child's voice, sweet and almost singing. 'There must be flowers for his grave, you see. Flowers for my head.'

The guard took the faded flower helplessly, but he did not move aside.

I needed to get into the palace *now*. My plan must be carried out in daylight. I could not risk the night. I slid down the wall till I rested on the stone floor, sitting in a froth of black silk skirts. Using the only other weapon in my quiver, I raised my voice and sang.

'*And will he not come again?*' My voice wavered. '*No, no, he is dead. Go to thy deathbed. He will never come again.*'

Footsteps. I forced myself to look at the blank wall, not at whoever came.

'Lady Ophelia?'

It was Horatio, Hamlet's friend. I almost trusted him. But if Hamlet had trusted him, why wasn't Horatio sailing to England with him? Every face at court might be an enemy now.

I lifted my head, but did not meet his eyes. '*He is dead and gone, lady,*' I sang. '*He is dead and gone …*'

'Lady Ophelia! My lady, look at me!'

I shook my head. 'I must tell the queen,' I said in my child's voice. 'Tell her he is dead, flowers for his grave there be, flowers for my head.' I looked at Horatio, my eyes wide.

'My father is dead. I must tell the queen my father is dead. *For he is dead and gone,*' I sang again.

'For the sake of all that is pitiful. Here, let me help you up, my lady.'

Horatio's hands were gentle on mine. I hated to trick a man who seemed so kind, but what honesty was there here at court?

'I will try to persuade the queen to see you,' Horatio said gently. 'Lady Ophelia, I will call the maids to tend you.'

'*Let in the maids,*' I sang. '*Then out a maid, never departed more ...*'

'Ahoy!' Horatio called. 'Tend us here!'

A footman peered at us, replaced quickly by some of the serving maids. Horatio beckoned them to take my arms as I flopped against his side. He left, and I began to sing again, softly, hoping he would come back soon. I had too little experience of madness to play this part for long.

At last more footsteps, then Horatio's gentle voice again. 'My lady, I have persuaded the queen to see you. Come, my lady.'

He took my arm, and one of the maids took the other. Between them they led me down the corridor, up the stairs and along another passage. I leaned my head this way and that, muttering and singing.

The doors to the throne room were already open. I glanced sideways. The queen sat on her throne, but the king's throne was empty. Lady Hilda, Lady Anna and

Lady Annika sat on their stools. Lady Annika seemed to be asleep as usual. The other two were busy with their needles.

Horatio let go of my hand, and bowed.

I ran forward before he could speak. 'Where is the beauteous Majesty of Denmark?'

The queen stared at me uncomfortably. 'How now, Ophelia?'

I twirled as if I danced in the snow, holding out my skirts. '*How should I your true love know, From another one?*' I sang. '*By his cockle hat and staff, And his sandal shoon.*'

Lady Annika's eyes opened, but she said nothing. The other ladies lifted their eyes from their sewing, then carefully looked back down.

'Alas, sweet lady, what imports this song?' There was true concern in the queen's voice.

She believes I am mad, I thought. It's working!

'Say you?' I said, keeping my voice childlike. 'Nay, pray you, listen.' I began to sing again. '*He is dead and gone, lady, He is dead and gone; At his head a grass-green turf, At his heels a stone.*'

The queen rose to her feet. 'Nay, but Ophelia —'

'*White his shroud as the mountain snow ...*'

I stopped as King Claudius strode into the room. The queen waited for him to step up onto the dais next to her.

'Alas, look here, my lord!' she said.

It took all the art I had to meet the king's eyes, to

smile at him with the sweetness and innocence of a rice pudding.

'*Larded with sweet flowers*,' I sang to him. '*Which bewept to the grave did go, With true-love showers*.'

Claudius looked at me warily. 'How are you, pretty lady?'

'Well, God give you what you deserve!' I told him earnestly. I leaned closer, and whispered as if it were a secret: 'They say the owl was a baker's daughter.' I stood straight again and picked a flower from my hair. I held it out to him. 'Lord, we know what we are, but know not what we may be. God be at your table!'

I could see the relief run across the king's face; it could almost have made a puddle at his feet. He took my poor dead flower automatically, rubbing it between his fingers.

'She is talking about her father,' he said.

I nodded stupidly. 'Pray you, let's have no words of this; but when they ask you what it means, say you this.' I began a song I had heard our laundress sing, careful to make it sound as if I did not know what the words meant:

'*Tomorrow is Saint Valentine's day,*
All in the morning betime,
And I a maid at your window,
To be your Valentine.
Then up he rose and donned his clothes
And opened the chamber door,
Let in the maid …'

I lowered my eyes, let anguish slip like a breeze across my face and then be gone.

'... *thut out a maid,*

Never departed more.'

'Pretty Ophelia!' The king almost sounded sorry for me. A girl abandoned by her lover, with no thought in her mind but how she had been despoiled. Perhaps he did feel pity. If a man might smile and be a villain, could a villain feel pity too?

'Indeed, I'll get to the end soon!' I said, and sang the second verse.

'*By Jesus and by Saint Charity,*

Alack, and fie for shame!

Young men will do it if they get a chance;

By Cock, they are to blame.

Said she, "Before you got me into bed,

You promised me to wed."

He answers,

"So would I have done, by yonder sun,

If you hadn't come to bed."'

It was as open a proclamation as if I had yelled it in the marketplace. Prince Hamlet has taken my virtue. He has killed my father, and then abandoned me. Not even the king could think I was a dangerous ally of his nephew now, nor fit to be a rebel with my brother.

Lady Anna and Lady Hilda looked carefully at their sewing. Gentlewomen did not speak of such things. Not unless they were mad indeed. I saw that Lady Annika's eyes were closed again.

'How long has she been like this?' demanded the king.

'I hope all will be well,' I said in my little girl voice. 'We must be patient; but I cannot help weeping when I think of him lying in the cold ground. My brother shall hear of this; and so I thank you for your good advice. Come, my coach! Good night, ladies. Good night, sweet ladies. Good night, good night.'

I twirled, my black skirt spinning out, once, twice, three times, then danced out of the throne room. I danced along the corridor, my hand out as if held by an invisible lover. I did not dare to look back to see if I was being watched.

I heard Horatio say something. Was he going to try to catch me? The queen's voice called him back. No, she would not want a mad girl kicking and screaming in the palace, shrieking out how Prince Hamlet had taken advantage of her, then killed her father. Best to let me leave the palace, go back to the seclusion of my house. Where else would she think I might go?

No other hand stopped me. It is bad luck to touch the mad. Servants hung back. The porter crossed himself and murmured a prayer, then hurried to open the palace door for me. I smiled at him as I danced down the palace stairs, and offered him a flower, dead and faded from my hair.

The palace was behind me now. I could hear muttering. Do not look back, I thought. Do not look back.

Through the palace courtyard, out into the marketplace. I turned to take the path towards the king's forest.

'Laertes for king! King Laertes! To death with Claudius the traitor! Laertes for king!' The cries still came from the far side of the marketplace.

I dared not hesitate. I did not want those who followed me to think I'd heard them. I twirled, still singing. People backed away from me and stared. Some muttered. Others laughed. I tried to look as if I heard nothing but my song.

'But he is gone, lady, but he is gone …'

Vaguely I was aware of eyes watching from the palace windows, voices shouting. But the rabble made too much noise to hear what they were saying.

'They bore him barefaced on the bier,' I sang. *'Hey, non nonny, nonny, hey nonny. And in his grave rained many a tear.'*

I ran up to a lavender-seller. She shrank away. 'Fare you well, my dove!' I called to her.

I skipped over to the firewood-seller. 'You must sing, *A-down a-down*, and you, *Call him a-down-a*. Oh, how the wheel becomes it!' I whispered at him. I sang again: *'It is the false steward that stole his master's daughter.'*

The man laughed nervously.

I twirled, feeling my skirts rush around me. The crowd drew back. I took a daisy from my hair and held it out. No one took it.

'There's rosemary, that's for remembrance. Pray you, love, remember.' I took another flower, looked at it sadly, then tossed it to a stout lady carrying a piglet. 'And there is pansies, that's for thoughts. There's fennel for you, and columbines.'

The piglet wriggled; it, at least, wanted the flowers. The woman held it firmly.

The marketplace was quiet now, all eyes on me. This is how you hide when all can see you, I thought. This is how a girl escapes her prison.

'There's rue for you, and here's some for me. We may call it herb of grace on Sundays. Oh, you must wear your rue with a difference! There's a daisy.'

I looked around the silent crowd. No obscene songs now. I wanted them to remember my words. If my brother did come to claim the throne, I wanted these people to remember how they had prospered with the guidance of my father.

'I would give you violets,' I said clearly, 'but they withered all when my father died. They say he made a good end.'

Men shuffled uncomfortably, remembering just what that end had been. Women whispered, pity in their eyes.

'Bonny sweet Robin is all my joy,' I whispered, almost to myself. I sang again:

'And will he not come again?
And will he not come again?
No, no, he is dead.
Go to thy deathbed.
He never will come again.
His beard was as white as snow
All flaxen was his poll.
He is gone, he is gone,
And we cast away moan.'

I slowly turned in circles, the last of my flowers gone. 'God have mercy on his soul. And on all Christian souls, I pray God. God be with you.'

I danced again, my hands holding up my skirts. I danced out through the marketplace and down the road. I danced and whirled past farmhouses. I danced into the forest, not twirling now as it made me giddy. I danced under the trees, danced like the leaf shadows, like the sunbeams, danced towards the glade.

And there, at the far end of the glade, gleamed the stream.

Chapter 20

I climbed the willow tree next to the stream, to wait till the watchers caught up with me. I knew they would come; sent by the king out of wariness, from Horatio or the queen out of pity. It mattered not except that they came.

I heard their voices, calling me. Two maids. Good. I had been afraid they might send a footman, who could swim.

I waited till I saw them run under the pine tree that I had stood beneath in the snow with Hamlet.

Then I fell.

The water grasped me, like a friend, eager to embrace me. I expected to sink at once, but the air trapped beneath my skirts held me up. I felt myself float along the stream. It was almost pleasant, giving myself up to the water. Was this what Hamlet had felt when he dreamed of ending his existence? That he might just float, and watch the sky?

'*Lady all a'dillo,*' I sang. '*Lay me down and cry ...*'

'Lady Ophelia!'

One of the maids stretched out her hand to save me. I could have grabbed it if I tried. Instead, I let the current carry me away, around the bend of the stream, where its banks were hidden by willow trees.

The water was cold. The women wailed upon the bank.

I was sinking now. The clothes that had borne me up dragged me down. Down, down … my shoulders under the water, then my neck. I held my face up to the air, breathed one last deep sweet sigh.

The water closed above me.

I forced my eyes open. Light shone above me: a green world, faintly bubbled. A brown world below. But not too far below.

I knew this stream, knew how deep it was. I felt my feet touch the bottom.

I needed to get out of my skirts. My lungs screamed as I struggled to free my legs. The skirts floated up, into that world of light and air.

Now for the sleeves, the shift. They wouldn't float. Let them be found on the river bed, muddy, sodden.

Let me be free.

I did not know how to swim. Who would teach a girl? But I had thought that if a person could walk along the land, she must be able to walk the same land underwater, as long as she could hold her breath. I hadn't realised it would be so hard, pushing against the stream that wanted to keep me down. The green above began to blacken. My lungs had no more air. I must go up. Go up or die!

I pushed my feet against the mud of the river bottom. My body speared up, towards the light. Air! I gulped it, like a child guzzling new milk. Sweet air, that smelled of trees and flowers and light.

I gulped three times more before I could look around.

The glade was gone. The women too. I heard them still wailing in the distance. Blessed willow trees that shielded me from their sight.

I was wet and friendless. But I was free.

Chapter 21

Free and cold. It took almost all my strength to wade to the bank, to clamber up. I lay there gasping, then forced myself to stand. The women had gone. I heard their wailing grow fainter and fainter still. But they would be back, with others to search the stream for my body. I must vanish before they came.

For the first time I was glad to be a girl. What else would a girl who had lost her virtue do but drown herself? It would not occur to anyone that she might survive a ducking in the stream. Especially not a mad girl. 'Pretty lady' King Claudius had called me, as if I were nothing but a flower.

An almost frozen flower now. My teeth chattered. My limbs were so numb I could hardly feel the grass, nor the nettles that stung my legs. I wanted to sink to the ground. But there was no time.

My body had never been bare to the air before. Sunlight prickled my skin. *Doubt that the sun doth move*, I thought. Dear friend, the sun.

I fumbled at the stockings tied around my waist. I managed to get the knots loose. The shirt was cold as well as wet. It clung to me. So did the breeches. Even with the stockings pulled up and gartered, the shoes on, my hair gathered up under the hat, I still looked ... wet. Conspicuous.

I could pass for a young man at night. But in daylight? With the wet shirt clinging to my bosom? Summer's darkness is too brief to hide for long. I must get away; let my clothes dry.

I ran into the forest as new voices yelled from the road. They would be here soon, with poles to find my body in the water and a door to bear me back on. They would not know how far the stream had carried me. I would have at least a week before anyone wondered why they couldn't find my body to settle in its grave.

Would they be generous and bury me in the churchyard? Or outside it, like the blacksmith's poor ruined daughter who had killed herself. Did a death caused by madness count as suicide?

But there wouldn't be a grave, I realised, as I found a tree the right shape and size, and grabbed its lowest branch to haul myself up. There was no body to put in it.

It was curiously peaceful up my tree. I tried to keep my mind off the cold and nettle stings, and listened to the yells of the searchers: a cry of triumph as someone found my clothes; mutters of disappointment when they found nothing else.

My clothes dried as sweet as washing on a line. Sitting on the branch in the dappled sunlight, I even began to feel warm. And hungry. I should have brought food. But what could I have packed in the stockings that the water would not have soaked? Cheese, I thought. I should have brought some cheese.

I had no cheese. No water either. I should have drunk from the stream when I'd had the chance. Would the search party never go?

The sun rolled down the sky and sat upon the trees. At last the searchers left, still muttering, my poor muddied clothes piled on the door they'd brought to carry away my body. More searchers would be here again tomorrow, I thought. But by then I would be gone.

I waited till the birds began to sing again as the intruders left their forest. Then I clambered down, causing them to lapse into silence again, and slipped through the trees to the road. I waited then, just inside the edge of the forest. I did not trust that I could find my way through trees in darkness, but I could find my way along a road by moonlight.

Time passed. Carts creaked along the road. Oxen bellowed in protest at their loads. Boys yelled and whipped at them with sticks.

A countrywoman passed, singing a song as bawdy as the one I'd sung to pretend madness. I peered out at her. She was Father's age, with grey hair under her cap. No burden — she must have sold her goods today. She carried nothing but the loaf of bread she chewed between

her verses, and perhaps some coins tied in her petticoat. I envied her the bread and her contentment. Envied her the freedom to sing a song with bawdy verses. Envied her the home she would be going to, with a bright fire, a pot on the hearth set by her daughter or daughter-in-law. A prosperous cottage, for she was well-fleshed. Winter had not left her hungry. No doubt she had pigs in the sty. And a family waiting for her.

I cried again, a little. For my father, for myself. Would I ever have a family now? If Laertes seized the throne, I would be coin for a royal alliance, like poor Hamlet. But if Laertes did not rebel? If Hamlet returned with an army? If ...

So many ifs. All I could do — like every other woman in the world, except those who were queens — was wait to see how the men disposed of the land, and us.

At last the road grew quiet. Night settled like a soft dark quilt across the land. Stars flickered in the velvet deep. *Doubt thou the stars are fire ...*

I thrust the memory away.

The moon rose: a goodly cheese, round and uncut. The stars faded in its light, as did the lamps' glow from the farmhouse across the way. I waited while the moon rose higher still. The palace would be asleep now, except the guards on the towers. They would be watching for an army, for men on horseback, for a rabble armed with rakes and scythes, not for one young man who knew the palace's walls and shadows. Where better to hide than in the place I knew like my own hand?

I had no chance of getting through the gate unseen. But my brother had told me of a spot in the wall with footholds, where young men climbed over when they wanted a night of dalliance. I found the place without trouble; put my feet in the crumbled stone, my hands in the holes above. I wondered how many generations this wall had served. It would be of no use to an invading army — too easy to pick off soldier after soldier climbing slowly up. But it was perfect for dallying young men. And me.

I half slid, half jumped down the wall on the other side. It was higher than I thought, and I fell, twisting my knee. It hurt, but I could still move. Must move, now, before I stiffened.

I did not make for the main palace door, of course, nor even the kitchen entrance, but for a tiny door on the other side, which was opened only in high summer, when the court left for the country and the privies were cleaned. I moved quickly, a shadow among shadows, trying to look as much like a servant on lawful duty as I could.

The door was unlocked. Why bolt a privy door? It was too narrow for an army to pass through it. Even my skirts would not have fitted.

The stench made me gag, but I was soon past it. Along the corridor, up the servants' staircase, past Lady Annika's robing room, where her dresses hung by the privy hole to keep the moths away. I hoped her servants slept as soundly as she did.

The old floors of the palace creaked. Rats gnawed at the wainscot. I must remind Lady Hilda to call the rat-catcher and his terriers, I thought automatically, then shrugged it away.

My stomach rumbled. But I could not risk going down to the kitchens tonight. It had taken me too long to get here. I risked meeting an early servant stoking up the breakfast fires, who might ask questions. One day without food and drink wouldn't kill me. Discovery might.

Along another corridor, then I was unlocking the tiny tower door. I shut the door behind me, and shut away my old life with it. I turned the key in the lock, put it in my pocket, then climbed the stairs. My childhood stairs, dear familiar tower stairs. I was safe.

I did not look around from the battlements tonight. Instead, I curled like a hedgehog on the second-highest of the steps, using the top one as a pillow. Hard stone, but away from the wind. At last I slept.

The sun woke me. I stretched. I remembered cold; the brief night sucking the heat from the palace walls, and me. I remembered warmth as daylight spread a blanket over me. Now I was too hot in the narrow staircase.

I rubbed my eyes, sat up. I didn't stand, in case someone saw movement on the little tower and wondered who was up here.

I needed a privy. I hadn't thought of that. A privy tower but no privy! Well, I would have to wait till tonight for that too. The privy was only next to my tower door, but too much chance that a servant might slip down the corridor to use it during the day. The palace would be bustling by now.

What was happening in the world outside?

Worry about yourself, not the kingdom, I told myself. Yesterday I had wanted only to find safety. I was as safe here as anywhere in the kingdom, now I was dead. And yet the kingdom's future was unravelling all around me. Denmark's fate might be as dismal as my own. I had to at least try to find out what was happening.

I couldn't risk standing up on the tower in daylight, but I could peek between the battlements. I edged my way across the tower on my knees, glad of the breeches not skirts, and peered between the stones.

Nothing. Or rather much, but nothing to sway a kingdom. No rabble calling for Laertes to be king today. No Hamlet marching upon the castle with an army. No rebellion. Just a guard relieving himself against a wall. My need for the privy grew.

Beyond the walls of the royal garden, the usual carters headed home, their loads delivered to the palace. Far-off tiny figures threw grain to even smaller hens. I smelled baking bread and my stomach growled again.

I crawled over to the other side of the battlements. I could see the road through the woods from here, the castle gate, even hear a porter making a joke to another. I could see the church and graveyard. There was my father's grave, newly filled. The flowers we had carried behind his coffin had wilted against the dark soil. It was almost company, seeing him there. Almost.

I glanced up at the main tower. Guards stood on sentry duty, as always. They probably couldn't see me, but it was silly to risk staying up here. Best go back down.

I crawled to the staircase, then climbed back down to the door. Few people used this little corridor, but just possibly, if I stayed with my ear to the door, I might overhear something that could tell me what was happening in the castle. A footman saying, 'We must polish the king's gauntlets — he is off to fight Laertes tomorrow.' Or 'Prince Hamlet's army is approaching.' I might even hear, 'The king is hunting deer tomorrow,' which would mean rebellion had been forgotten. Or perhaps two maids might stop to gossip …

I halted near the bottom of the stairs, and stared. There, inside the shut door, was a flask; a plate piled with rye bread, white sheep's cheese flecked with herbs, and pickled herring; a folded man's cloak; and, wondrous as a shooting star, a chamberpot politely covered with a thick cloth.

My first reaction was a wave of hunger and relief. My second: danger. That was a locked door! I checked my pocket. Yes, I still had the key.

Cautious now, I tiptoed down the last steps and over to the door, in case anyone waited beyond it, and tried the handle. Locked, as I had left it. Yet there was the plate, the flask, that lovely chamberpot.

I used it first, covered it with the cloth, then carried my meal up to the top of the stairs. I used the cloak as a cushion. I drank the small ale — it was good new ale; sweet, not sour — then slowly ate every speck of bread and cheese and herring, and licked my fingers till even the scent was gone.

Fresh bread. Sheep's cheese from three years ago, I thought, at its peak; its flavour matured but not crumbly with age. The herring had been lightly pickled with dill and juniper. Who could have brought it?

Gerda, I thought. She must have followed me to the tower one night. Many nights, perhaps. Gerda was loyal to me. Perhaps she'd guessed I might come here. But how had she got a key? Most doors had more than one key, but even if Gerda knew where spare keys hung in the palace, she wouldn't have known which one to take. Besides that, I suspected the guards would be keeping my servants confined to our house, in case they ran to join my brother.

Could Queen Gertrude have arranged this? She was fond of me, I knew, fond almost as a mother. Nor, despite Hamlet's ravings, could I think of her as guilty as he judged her. She had shown only bewilderment when the king had raged off during the play. The queen was skilled at hiding her feelings, like everyone at court, but I did not think she could pretend as well as that.

Had someone seen me come in here last night and reported it to the queen? I thought back. I was sure I had not been seen. And why should Queen Gertrude help me now, when she had ignored me in my sorrow after Father's death?

Yet someone who knew my habits must have guessed I might be here. Someone who had a key, had opened the door, crept up the stairs and seen me as I slept. Horror crawled along my arms and legs. They could have killed me. Fool, to think I was safe here.

No, I *was* safe. There had been no knife stabbing me in the darkness, just a gift of food and drink, a cloak and a chamberpot.

Was it the ghost of old King Fortinbras? I smiled at myself. King Fortinbras wouldn't think of a chamberpot either, even if a ghost could spirit up bread and cheese and herring. No, a real friend, of bones and blood.

That chamberpot told me much about my secret friend. A jailer might think of food and water. Laertes, if he were here, if he had heard somehow from our servants where I might be found, might have ordered someone to bring me cheese and ale. Horatio might have too. But not a chamberpot, with a cloth to stop it stinking. Men never thought of such things. My friend must be a woman.

I had a friend. I hugged the thought to me, warmer than the cloak on which I sat. Perhaps I should not venture out to find more food and drink tonight, but let my friend help me.

Time enough to think of that. I took the plate back to the door, then climbed the stairs again. And slept.

Chapter 22

It was late when I woke. Now, so close to midsummer, the sun lingered long after honest folk had eaten their suppers. I peered cautiously between the stones of the battlements. There was no one to be seen, except a porter sweeping the day's horse, goat and sheep droppings from the castle courtyard, and an ancient beggar picking her way around the market square, hoping for a dropped bun or turnip or a farthing lost among the cabbage leaves. I crept back into the stairwell, then stopped.

A noise, below. A rat? No, the clinking of a key.

I hesitated only a moment. If it was my unknown friend, I had nothing to fear. If not, I would pretend to be a lad coming down from admiring the view from the tower. 'Key?' I'd say. 'What key?' And then I'd run.

I rounded the last corner of the staircase as the door shut. The key scraped in the lock. I fumbled for my own key, tied in a corner of my shirt. I slid it in, trying to hear any movement outside. Footsteps, the swish of cloth …

At last I got the door open. I peered out, just as a skirt vanished around a corner into another corridor.

I stepped back quickly and locked the door again. It was a woman; I had been right. The corridor had been too dim to see the skirt clearly. It could have been silk or wool; queen or washerwoman.

I looked at what she had brought me. A closed pot of what smelled like fish soup. More bread, a hunk of aged Summer Mountain cheese, a small bowl of strawberries. Strawberries! Not a washerwoman then. Nor Gerda. No one in our house could have gone berrying in the forest, and to buy berries like these would have cost a silver piece.

The chamberpot sat where I had left it. I lifted up the cloth. Empty. For a second I thought it was enchanted. A ghost had spirited away the mess I'd left there. Then sense took over. This must be another pot, the other taken away. One chamberpot looked like any other. Even the queen's was plain white china.

Her Majesty would not carry a chamberpot. But she had trusted maids who might. The queen need not even tell the maid why she must go to the small cupboard in the dusty corridor and leave food and a chamberpot. Queens were obeyed, not questioned, even if their excuse was thin. Who else could have brought me strawberries? Maybe she had not called me to her after my father's death because she thought being in the chamber where my father had been murdered would hurt me.

It had been my father, I realised, who had warned me that Hamlet might have to make a diplomatic marriage, not Queen Gertrude. She might have thought — with reason — that this stranger son, so long a foreigner to his people, might do best with a bride from a family the people knew and trusted. She might have truly wanted me to be her daughter. Perhaps she hoped it still.

I slept the next night out on the battlements, wrapped in the cloak; it was all I needed in the summer warmth. Its cloth was dark enough to hide me. Whoever had left it for me had thought of that too.

I hoped rather than expected more food to be at the bottom of the staircase when I woke. It was. Bread and cheese — sheep's milk again. Did whoever left it know I didn't like goat's milk cheese? And more fresh-made ale, with a small pot of stewed cherries. And this time, a ewer of water and a washcloth.

Two women brought all this, I thought, not one; unless she made two trips.

I realised something else too. My provisions came only when I was safely up above. Someone watched my tower.

Whoever my friend was, she didn't want me to know her identity. How easy to call up to me: 'Lady Ophelia! Your food is here.' Or even, if she had been given orders and did not know my name: 'Kind sir, do not let the ale go cold.' But she came in secret. Knew my secret too. I had never told anyone that I came here, not since I had told my nurse about King Fortinbras, so many years ago. I had told no one I intended to hide. How could they know?

I shivered. Only ghosts could know I was here. The ghost of Hamlet's father, who must truly walk these battlements. Old Fortinbras's ghost. Did the two old enemies meet each other now, on top of the castle?

But ghosts did not carry chamberpots, nor rye bread. Nor could they hurt the living, except by poisoning their minds.

Poor Hamlet, pushed and harried by his father's ghost. *Doubt that the sun doth move; doubt truth to be a liar; but never doubt I love.*

I clenched my fists with sudden resolution. I could do one thing, at least, hidden up here. I could summon the old king's ghost tonight.

That, at least, I owed to Hamlet.

The midsummer sky was grey above me, just dark enough for pale stars to struggle through. I sat against the stones and hugged my cloak around me. I could just make out the watch on the main tower, their dark armoured silhouettes against the sky. An owl hooted in the forest nearby. Some poor creature shrilled its death; another owl's meal. I tried to count the stars to pass the time, but gave up as clouds drifted past them like Lady Annika's lace shawl. Surely it was gone midnight.

'King Hamlet!' My voice was low, but loud enough to call a ghost.

No answer.

I tried again. 'King Hamlet! It is I, your son's friend, who calls you.'

The battlements showed a distinct absence of ghostly king.

'King Hamlet!'

No answer. Perhaps summer's darkness was too thin for a ghost to appear. Did ghosts get bored in summer, with so few black hours when they could haunt?

I called again, and again. I called till the moon hid behind a shawl of cloud. My eyes began to close ... The clouds thickened into shape. A man peered at me. No, not a man — a ghost. He wore the same crown that now King Claudius wore, with the gold doublet and hose I had seen the old king wear, though both were grey now. Even their embroidery was grey. The black and white beard was grey too. His grey eyes that had once been blue stared at my face.

I scrambled to my feet. I tried to curtsey, then found I had no skirts to hold. I made a clumsy bow instead. 'Your Majesty.'

He floated further off and still said nothing. Even as I watched, he began to fade. Would he speak only to his son?

'Your Majesty,' I said urgently, 'I am Ophelia, your son's affianced wife.'

Was I? I wasn't sure. Officially I was dead, and Hamlet exiled. There had been no bridal contracts planned. But the ghost heard enough truth in my voice to float closer.

I should be scared, I thought. I had always been nervous around the old king, a man who threw his baked carp at a servant because the sauce was too sweet, then had the man hung by his thumbs for three days. Sometimes I still dreamed of his screams. A man who watched his hounds rip open a deer's throat; while the deer's blood flowed, at least the rest of us were safe. But even a mortal girl is stronger than a ghostly king.

'Remember me!' The ghostly voice was hoarse, but still that of the king I'd known.

'I remember you,' I said.

The grey crowned head loomed above me. 'I am thy Hamlet's father's spirit, doomed for a certain term to walk the night, confined all day to waste in fires, till the foul crimes I have done are burned and purged away.'

'I know,' I said.

It was as if he hadn't heard. 'But fouler still the crime done to me. Murdered, by a brother's hand. Oh, horrible! Oh, horrible! Most horrible. The royal bed of Denmark now a couch for damned incest —'

I raised my voice to speak over him. 'I know all about that.'

He stared at me. Had anyone ever interrupted him before, as king or ghost?

'Attend me well,' he whispered harshly. 'For you must help to avenge what you will hear —'

'You are going to tell me that your brother poured poison in your ear while you slept. And your wife then married him.'

'Yes! Foul and poisonous incest.'

'But what *you* don't know,' I said, 'is that your son is sent across the sea to England, where he may be killed.'

He floated a little further away. 'What is it you say?'

'Your son is in danger. Might lose his life. Has lost all happiness because of you.'

He loomed above me again, the far-off stars shining like red points of anger in his eyes. 'How dare a girl speak to me this way!'

I put my hands on my hips. 'I had a father once, but not like you. If my father's ghost should walk — which it will not, for he was a good man and sits now in heaven — he would give his children words of wise counsel, treasures dropped from years of wisdom, not bluster of revenge.'

'You dare to argue with me!'

'I do! Why did your wife so quickly turn to your brother for comfort? Why did Denmark's lords accept him as king?'

He swooped around me, his ghostly hands stretched out as if to wring my neck. I did not flinch. Those fingers had less strength than mist.

He kept circling, so close I felt I breathed in his cloud. Was he trying to make me fall off the battlements? I would not back down.

At last he surged a little way beyond the tower. The dim sparkle of his eyes glared at me. 'I am the king!' he howled.

'You *were* the king. And so was King Fortinbras, whose kingdom you took as a prize for a bet. Does King Fortinbras torment his son like this?'

His eyes blazed silver from his shades of grey. 'I must have revenge!'

'Why?'

'Murder is foul, most foul, unnatural —'

'So is a ghost who torments his son.' I stepped towards the ghost, my toes at the edge of the battlements. I could feel the updraught of the warm stones below. 'Promise me you will not torment your son when he returns. Leave him in peace, and your kingdom too. Promise me!'

'I must be —'

I fixed him with a glare. 'All you must be, Your Majesty, is burned in fires each day, as you have said, for your sins. Would you add to your life's sins after death by hurting those who act from duty and love of you? One person loved you — one only — and you torment him! Save yourself a day, a year, of sulphurous flames and leave your son alone.'

'A girl to so assault me! A very shrew.' The ghostly voice was almost sulky.

'Go,' I said. 'And may heaven send you finally to rest.'

He floated beyond the battlements, slowly fading. I thought I heard one last 'Remember me.' But it might only have been the wind.

Chapter 23

King Hamlet's ghost did not haunt my tower again. Nor did the people cry out Laertes's name.

Fear and boredom mixed make the worst of potions. I slept. I used the chamberpot. I ate and drank, and was grateful to my unknown benefactor for all. Try as I might, I could not catch her at it. At last I accepted that trying to was poor gratitude for her generosity.

I watched the life of the town and castle from the battlements. Egg-sellers came to market, and men with loads of hay; a herd of geese was driven up the road, destined for the palace kitchens. The king and queen led the court past the quiet graveyard to church, and back again. The queen sat in the royal garden, while her ladies stitched.

Once, the king rode out to hunt, returning with stag and wild boar. At least, I thought, that means he doesn't expect to run into a rebel army led by Laertes, or an English army with Hamlet at its head. There was venison on my bread the next morning, but that told me nothing of who had brought it. Lords, ladies and servants alike ate the king's leftovers.

I was almost used to sleeping in the stairway now. Inactivity was harder. I sat and thought. I dozed and watched. Night and day made little difference. Mostly, I watched the marketplace, the palace gates. In the quiet times, I watched the royal garden, remembering how I had first met Hamlet there. I gazed at the graveyard too, thinking of my father, how Hamlet had killed him with no more compassion than if he'd killed a rat.

Today was not a market day. All the deliveries to the palace were done by the time its clock chimed nine. A mob of children played tag about the square, squealing and laughing. They were barefoot, in rags, but apple-cheeked, well-fed. They would not laugh if war came to Denmark. Rebellions could last for years. Fields would grow weeds because their farmers were bearing swords, not ploughs. Pigsties would go untended ...

A woman called, and the children ran inside a cottage just outside the castle walls. The marketplace was strangely quiet, and the road too, quieter even than a Sunday. I turned to look out the other side of the tower, and saw my brother.

He was kneeling beside my father's grave; dressed in black velvet, not travelling clothes, there on the grass in quiet prayer. After a time, he stood and made his way slowly back into the palace.

I leaned against the tower stones, stunned. How long had Laertes been in Denmark? I had been so sure he would arrive with an army, or call the lords to war. Perhaps even as I played mad, he was riding up to our front door.

Was Laertes my unknown friend? No, surely not. He would have told me to come home. Because if he was safe at Elsinore, so was his sister. I could creep back to my rooms and find a dress, make myself known. There was no danger now.

Or was there? Laertes knew nothing of King Claudius's crimes, but I did — and the king knew it. Would I put Laertes in danger if I reappeared?

Even as I thought it, two men entered the graveyard carrying spades. They began to dig what could only be a grave, close to my father's, but beyond the churchyard fence. My heart beat louder than a drum. Was the new grave for my brother? Had Laertes rebelled, been captured, paroled to say his prayers at Father's grave, and was now to be executed, cast into unsanctified ground?

No. I had never seen a rebellion, but I suspected they caused fuss. The biggest fuss I had seen from my tower had been a cackling herd of geese.

I lay flat on the stones, watching the gravediggers as I tried to work out what must have happened. How had I missed Laertes's arrival? He must have been hailed by all those who called for him to be king. How could I have missed that? He must have arrived when I was pretending to be mad. He must believe his sister dead, and by her own hand. Dead for love; my madness caused by Hamlet's unfaithfulness and his murder of my father.

Laertes must have accepted the king's word that Hamlet had killed our father. Why should he not? For indeed that was what had happened.

I must go to my brother. I had caused him pain too long. But not in daylight, when someone might see me in boy's clothes and make the scandal worse. I would go tonight, creep along the corridor, scratch at his chamber door. I would tell him everything: how Hamlet had pretended to be mad; how Claudius had poisoned the old king; how I had faked my drowning. I would look to him for guidance.

Perhaps my pretended madness would serve us well. The king could pass off anything I said now as madness too. That made me safe. I could leave Elsinore. Leave all the plots behind. Stay at our estates a season, and then, when memories had faded, I could marry perhaps. Or count cabbages if no man was willing to marry Prince Hamlet's leavings, a girl who once was mad. Crabbed and confined my life would be, but what chance had I ever had of much else? Except my dream, once, to be a queen.

And Hamlet? Perhaps he was already dead at the English king's hand, as King Claudius had demanded. Perhaps he languished at the English court, pleading for the army that surely no wise king would give him. If the English king wanted Denmark, he could lead his own army here. He had no need of Hamlet, cast out of his own land for the murder of his lord chancellor, tainted with madness. Poor Hamlet.

My hand froze to the stones. For just as I thought his name, there he was, walking through the churchyard gates with Horatio.

He wore travelling clothes but carried no luggage, nor were his men with him. He was entering the castle grounds discreetly, via the churchyard, not by the main entrance. But he must surely know he would be seen.

Even as I watched, he stopped to talk with the gravediggers. He seemed strangely smaller, dimmer, than the man I had known. Had I given him false glamour, imagined him to be the prince I dreamed of? Or had the last months' troubles worn him away, as water washes away the soil after the grass has been eaten by too many goats?

I tried to see his face, read his demeanour. He seemed to jest with the gravediggers. He threw a ball into the air and grabbed it, grinning.

I caught my breath. That was not a ball. It was a skull.

Not a black mood then, but a too-merry one. How could a man joke with death so close to my father's grave? Not to mention the grave of the poor wretch who had their skull dug up today. I shivered. The last shreds of my love blew away with the wind. I could pity Hamlet. I could not love a man who played with death.

Movement caught my eye, by the palace stairs. A procession emerged. Laertes and three of his friends carried a coffin between them. Behind them came the king and queen, her arm on his. They were followed by the ladies and gentlemen of the court, in solemn black, the women scattering flowers.

Who was in that coffin that Laertes carried so grimly, with such ceremony? Who was to be buried outside the churchyard, but so near my father's grave?

And then I realised.

It was me.

Chapter 24

Who looks closely at a drowned body that the fish and eels have nibbled for over a week? Not my brother, and certainly not the queen. They had looked for Ophelia's body in the water. They had found a body, so it must be her.

'The river is where all bad girls go to be cleansed,' Gerda had told me. 'Death cleans all.' I shuddered. What poor girl lay in that coffin? Had her family thrown her out? Her lover spurned her? At least she would have a grave now.

Or perhaps it was not a girl. Perhaps a beggar, old and feeble, had fallen in the stream. A cut-throat might have tried to hide the body of his victim in the river. The king should use our troops to hunt down cut-throats, I thought, instead of attending the court to make a goodly show.

I stared at the king below me, the queen, the funeral procession. Part of me wanted to call out, 'Grieve not! I am here.' But the scandal would last a hundred years. 'Do you remember Lady Ophelia, who cried out at her own funeral?' people would say. 'Dressed as a boy, showing her legs and all!' No. I must keep to my plan. Go to my brother quietly tonight, so we could work out the safest way for me to reappear.

The church bell tolled once. Once for a woman, twice for a man. It began to toll again, marking the years of my life: one, two, three ...

Hamlet and Horatio stepped back behind one of the larger gravestones. The funeral procession reached the grave just as the sixteenth bell rang out. Its echoes shuddered across the graveyard. Even the crows in the yew trees were quiet now.

The pallbearers strapped ropes around the coffin, and lowered it into the grave. The priest took out his book. His words floated up to me from the silence of the graveyard. Even the marketplace behind me was silent. The kingdom knows the court is in mourning today, I thought. That is why it is so quiet. Even the horses' feet will be muffled, just as when the old king died.

Queen Gertrude and King Claudius stood side by side, their ladies and lords behind them. The queen wore black, looking more sombre than she ever had after her first husband's death. The king wore black as well: black clothes, black shadows under his eyes. He seemed almost skeletal, as if worms were eating at him from inside.

Was it guilt? Were the pressures of kingship heavier than he had thought? Did King Claudius worry that Laertes might lead a revolt; that Gertrude might discover his plot to kill her son?

The priest's words ended. He crossed himself, then stepped back from the grave.

My brother put his hand on the priest's arm. 'Surely you can give her more ceremony than this?' His words were faint, but clear.

The priest shrugged. 'Her death will always be suspicious. All we can do is this: her virgin rights, the bell and burial.'

'Can't you do more for her?' Laertes cried.

My heart tore at his anguish.

The priest lifted his chin. He would prefer to see me in an unmarked grave, I thought, buried at night, to shame my sin.

'No more can be done,' he said firmly. 'We should profane the service of the dead to sing a requiem and give such rest to her as to peace-departed souls.'

I thought Laertes might strike him.

'Lay her in the earth,' my brother ordered, each word cold and distinct. 'And from her fair and unpolluted flesh may violets spring! I tell you, churlish priest,' he made the word sound like an insult, 'my sister will be an angel in heaven when you lie howling below.'

The queen stepped forward quickly. She laid a hand on Laertes's shoulder; of comfort and, I thought, restraint.

'Sweets to the sweet,' she said, looking towards the coffin in the grave. 'Farewell.'

Lady Annika handed her a bunch of flowers. The queen scattered them into the dark hole.

'I thought I should have seen you Hamlet's wife,' she added, and her voice broke. 'I hoped to scatter flowers on your wedding bed, sweet maid, not on your grave.'

The stones themselves were not as cold as I. Had Queen Gertrude really wanted me to be Hamlet's wife? Or was it said merely to appease Laertes?

Her grief was real; I could see it by the way she turned her face away, to let the tears run from her eyes unseen. Queens did not cry, or not in public.

Laertes stared at the flower-covered coffin. 'May treble woe, ten times treble, fall on that cursed head whose wicked deed deprived you of your sense!' he said. All at once he leaped into the grave. I heard his feet thud on the coffin. 'Stop throwing in the earth,' he shouted, 'till I have caught my sister once more in my arms! Then pile it upon the quick and the dead.'

I held my breath. If Laertes wrenched the coffin open now, he would see it wasn't me. I wondered what would be more scandalous: my brother shouting, 'This is not my sister's body! Where is my sister?' or me, shrieking down at him, 'I am up here!'

'Who yells so in such grief?' Hamlet asked, advancing across the churchyard. He gazed at the astounded faces: his mother's, breaking into sudden joy; the king looking as if a wolf had bitten him; the courtiers staring open-mouthed.

'Yes, it is I!' Hamlet announced, with more dramatic flourish than any of the actors in his play. 'I, Hamlet the Dane!' He leaped into the grave too.

Wonderful, I thought. Three in a grave, and not one of them the person who is meant to be there.

'The devil take your soul!' shouted Laertes. He grabbed Hamlet by the throat.

Hamlet thrust my brother's hands away. 'Take off your hands! Though I am not angry or rash, yet I have something dangerous in me which you should fear.'

'Part them!' shouted the king.

The queen pressed her hand to her heart. 'Hamlet!' she cried.

Horatio bent down into the grave and grabbed Hamlet's arm. A couple of courtiers slid down and held back my brother.

'Good, my lord, be quiet,' panted Horatio.

Hamlet scrambled out of the grave. No man can look dignified, I thought, scrabbling in the dirt. He glared down at Laertes. 'I will fight you on this issue till my eyelids no longer wag.'

'My son, what issue is that?' cried the queen.

'I loved Ophelia!' Hamlet shouted. 'Forty thousand brothers could not, with all their quantity of love, make up my sum. What can you do for her?'

The king moved closer to my brother as he also scrambled out of the grave. 'He is mad, Laertes.' The king looked like a man in shock, trying to hold himself together.

'For the love of God, be patient with him,' pleaded the queen.

She put her hand on Hamlet's arm. He hardly noticed her. He stared at my brother, his voice raised to a scream.

'Would you weep for her? Would you fight? Would you fast? Would you tear yourself? Eat a crocodile? I'll do it!'

I couldn't see how eating a crocodile would prove he loved me. The one thing Hamlet could have done, but hadn't, was to speak to my father and claim me, in the eyes of God and of the court. Had he not done that to save me from the enmity of the king? Or was it to keep open the page of history that said, 'Prince Hamlet married an English princess, and then became the king of Denmark'? Hamlet hadn't even had the honesty or compassion to tell me why he did not marry me.

The queen looked pleadingly at the king, then at Laertes. 'This is only madness.'

I agreed. No one had asked Hamlet to eat a crocodile. Where would he even get one? It was as melodramatic as pouring poison in someone's ear.

Just shed a few tears for me, I thought, almost forgetting I wasn't really dead. Is that too much to ask?

The queen whispered to the king. I strained to listen. But the courtiers were speaking now, and Laertes was yelling, and Hamlet too, and poor Horatio was still trying to calm Hamlet down. The sounds were too muddled for me to make out what anyone was saying.

Slowly, the crowd moved away, back to the castle. Horatio guided Hamlet, who was still shouting. The king and queen stood either side of my brother, as if to stop him strangling his prince.

So much for my funeral.

Chapter 25

I sat back on the tower's stones. So both my brother and Hamlet loved me? Ha! If they loved me so much, they should have wept, not fought each other. Even Laertes had seemed to care more about punching Hamlet's nose than remembering me. I had thought my brother a sensible man, like our father.

But Hamlet had killed our father. And Laertes believed Hamlet had been the cause of my death too. Laertes had cause for anger. But Hamlet? Screaming and making a scene because my brother gave way to his grief. Offering to eat a crocodile!

Suddenly I grinned. It was ridiculous. Crocodile probably tasted quite good if cooked well, with a cream sauce and chives. Was Hamlet still pretending to be mad? Or were his ravings a sign of guilt, a whisper of true insanity? Both mixed together, I decided. Perhaps pretending to be a madman had loosened Hamlet's own behaviour and now it could not be put back.

At least both my brother and Hamlet were alive and free, not cast into a dungeon.

My time in my tower had come to an end too. I must go to our house to see my brother before he got into worse trouble. King Claudius would be all too happy if my brother killed Hamlet. Then Laertes could be tried for treason and executed, and both challengers to the king's throne would be gone.

I ran down the stairs. I fumbled for the key as a cry came from outside.

'A duel! A duel! Prince Hamlet fights Lord Laertes!'

I muttered an oath at the stupidity of men, and a curse on all rapiers. I ran back up to the battlements and peered over the edge. I didn't care if the guards saw me now. But the men on the other towers were all staring down too.

The court had gathered in the royal garden. Two chairs had been carried out for the king and queen, and stools for the ladies, and a table with wine and goblets laid on it. Laertes and Hamlet faced each other, rapiers in their hands. They were going to fight a duel! What would Father have said?

That young men must have their folly, I thought. And a duel, fought according to proper rules, might cool their tempers. The presence of the king and queen showed this was a formal duel, not a fight to the death. Each would try to land a point upon the other, with buttons covering the sharp ends of their rapiers. There would be no blood. A winner would be declared, and it would be done.

I could not think of a more foolish way to quarrel, nor pass the time — except, perhaps, torturing some poor bear to make it dance. At least when men hunted, they brought back food. But playing at fighting? Ridiculous.

I hugged the nearest stone. I would watch till the game was over, then seek out Laertes. I would tell him he was a fool to let himself be caught in the king's net, playing games with rapiers. I would convince him we should leave the court with its plots, and go to our estates to tend our lands and people. I would tell him it was time to think about what mattered, instead of frittering his life away with mistresses and duels.

The king settled in his seat. 'Cousin Hamlet,' he called, 'you know the wager?'

They were betting on a duel not an hour after my funeral? If I'd had a crocodile to hand, I would have shoved it in Hamlet's mouth. Without cream sauce. As for my supposedly grief-stricken brother …

'Very well, my lord,' answered Hamlet. He almost seemed happy, nursing his rapier confidently, a man who thought he would win. 'Your Grace has laid the odds on the weaker side.'

So the king had bet on my brother. He would probably win his bet, I thought. Just as his brother had won a bet in this very garden so many years ago.

Laertes lifted his rapier. 'This is too heavy. Let me see another.'

Hamlet weighed his in his hand. 'I like this one. Are all the blades the same length?'

The king's servant handed Laertes a different sword.

Queen Gertrude sat back, the most relaxed I had seen her since before her husband's death. Her smile reassured me. Had she been the one to suggest this duel? Duels were stupid, but men took them seriously. Perhaps it might mend the rift between Hamlet and Laertes. The queen knew what she was doing. Hamlet and Laertes would probably be toasting each other, the best of friends, by nightfall.

And if my brother's grief for me hadn't lasted very long, then hopefully it wouldn't shock him too much to find me alive.

And annoyed. If Laertes thought he could tell me what to do after this, he'd have to think again. To think I had believed him wise! I'd get him away from court and back to our estates if I had to drag him by the stockings. Or put poppy juice in his ale, and have him carted off, asleep.

But no matter what happened in the garden this morning, King Claudius was still a murderer. And Hamlet would still seek revenge.

Hamlet might not be mad as he had pretended. But nor was he … sensible. I thought of the fury of his speech in the library, when he thought I had betrayed him; his frantic glee at the play; even the too-fervent grief just now, over what he thought was my dead body, attacking my brother simply for showing his love for me.

No matter how I tried to twist it, I could never think of Hamlet as a good king for Denmark. He was a child, playing at plots, like he played with his sword below, his grief for me vanishing with the prospect of some sport.

Were any in Hamlet's father's family truly sane? I thought of the old king shrieking for revenge; King Claudius pouring poison in his brother's ear instead of discreetly slipping it into his wine. Hamlet was indeed his father's son. No matter what was going on between him and his uncle, Laertes and I and our household were best away from Elsinore.

'Come, sir!' cried Hamlet. He saluted Laertes with his rapier.

Laertes saluted him back. And lunged.

Hamlet laughed, parrying with his own weapon.

A few of the lords clapped. Ladies giggled, like trilling birds.

I didn't want to watch. Who cared who won or lost the bet? But I needed to see how King Claudius dealt with the duellists when their match was over. Would Hamlet be accepted as the king's heir again? Did the king trust Laertes enough to let us leave the court without wondering if Laertes did so to gather an army on our estates?

My brother lunged again, and then twice more. Hamlet parried them all.

More applause. Hamlet grinned, and bowed to the audience. He fenced better than I'd thought he would. Better than my brother and the king had thought too. This scholar had been practising.

All at once Hamlet's arm flashed forward. The tip of his foil touched Laertes's shirt.

'A hit! A very palpable hit!' cried someone. The audience cheered.

A woman plucked a flower from her hair and threw it towards Hamlet. He saw it, nodded to her and smiled.

The king grinned a reluctant acknowledgment. He lifted his goblet. 'To Hamlet! This drink is yours.'

He nodded to his servant to give Hamlet a goblet of wine too.

The queen smiled.

Yes, I thought, it was you who organised this. If Laertes and Hamlet settle their quarrel, my father's murder can be forgotten. Poor, careful Father. But I knew he would not call for revenge. If forgetting him meant peace in Denmark, Father would lie in his grave content.

Hamlet waved the wine away. 'I'll play this bout first,' he called to the king. 'Come,' he said to Laertes, 'another hit. What do you say?'

Had the court watched Hamlet's father fight King Fortinbras all those years ago? They must have. A kingdom's fate had rested on two thin swords. Goose-girls, wood-cutters, a kingdom's crops and cheeses, all dependent on who could prick the other with a sword.

The rapiers clashed again.

'A hit, I do confess!' called Laertes.

The king leaned over to the queen. 'Our son shall win,' he said loudly.

So he's your son now, I thought.

The queen smiled. 'Our son is fat and out of breath. Here, Hamlet, take my napkin and wipe your brow.' She lifted his goblet of wine to toast him. 'The queen drinks to your good luck, Hamlet.'

'Gertrude, do not drink!' The king grabbed at her arm, too late. The queen drank down the wine.

I frowned. Why shouldn't the queen drink?

She was already smiling an apology at the king. She said something to him, too low for me to hear. She blew him a kiss, then held the goblet of wine out to Hamlet again.

He shook his head. 'I will not drink it yet, madam.'

'Come, let me wipe your face,' she insisted.

He hesitated, then walked to her and kneeled by her chair. She smiled down at him as Lady Annika passed her a silk handkerchief, then she wiped his forehead tenderly, as if he were a baby. Hamlet met her eyes. Slowly, he smiled back. A cooing whisper ran around the watching court.

She has done it, I thought. Oh, clever queen. Hamlet has forgiven her. This duel would settle his enmity with Laertes. And even King Claudius seemed on good enough terms with Hamlet now. Maybe life would return to normal.

I should leave now, while everyone was watching the duel, and climb back into my skirts. I could be waiting for Laertes when he returned, and share with him a little of the truth: that I had been scared and had hidden till he returned.

Perhaps, instead of fleeing, I would find myself a lady-in-waiting again. Queen Gertrude had declared publicly that she had hoped I would be her daughter. It would be a cruel trick of fate if she announced me as Hamlet's bride just when I no longer wanted to be. I did not love him any more. Did not respect him.

But the queen had lived for a quarter-century with a man she did not love, had perhaps even hated. Could I do the same? Men gave their lives for their country. Women gave their lives for men, for their family. And for a queen, a family may be a whole kingdom wide.

I would think of it tomorrow. Tomorrow I would be a girl again, in my skirts. I would have a bed, a bath, a brother who loved me, even if not as extravagantly as he claimed ... Why did I feel like crying? I wiped the tears away angrily. Time to go back to my real life.

Hamlet raised his rapier. 'Come for a third hit, Laertes!' he yelled. 'You are dallying.'

Laertes slashed towards him, fast. 'Have at you now!'

Hamlet stepped back. A small rose bloomed upon his shoulder. Blood.

Someone screamed.

I leaned over the battlements. There should be no blood in a duel like this. Someone had taken the buttons off the rapiers! This was no play fight. My brother and my lover were fighting to the death.

Men's voices rose, angry and alarmed. Women chattered like starlings in a tree. But no one stepped in to part the duellists.

Hamlet stared at the blood spreading across his shirt. He gazed fiercely at Laertes for a second as long as winter, then grasped his rapier again. His sword crashed against Laertes's. They struggled for a moment, neither giving way, forcing the rapiers from each other's hands. Both their weapons clattered to the paving. They grabbed them up again. I saw that Laertes had taken Hamlet's rapier, and Laertes Hamlet's. I doubted either noticed.

Another rose grew red, this time on Laertes's arm.

Someone stop them, I thought desperately, just as Claudius yelled: 'Separate them! They are incensed!'

Hamlet and Laertes took no notice. Their world had narrowed to their swords, to each other, and to their hatred.

Horatio tried to grab Hamlet's arm. Hamlet thrust him away, still circling Laertes.

I had to stop them! I was the only one who could. Once they saw I was alive, they'd have to stop. If I was alive, Laertes could not blame Hamlet for my death. He might even accept that our father's death was an accident, if I told him so. And if Hamlet was willing to eat a crocodile for me, the least he could do was put down his rapier.

I clattered down the stairs, fumbled for the key. The door swung open.

I ran along the corridor, down the stairs, across the central courtyard, then into the wing near the royal garden. No one stopped me. No one even saw me. Every servant must be watching the duel from some window or tower. They would see me too, wearing boy's clothes, revealing myself as a woman. A scandal. Well, I could survive scandal. What was a queen but a woman who knew her own mind and made men follow her? I might never wear a crown, nor even have a husband, but I could stop two men killing each other today.

The garden door was open. Servants clustered around. I elbowed my way through them, under shoulders.

Clack! Snick! Clack! The two figures lunged around the garden. Half of Hamlet's shirt was red with blood. Red dripped from Laertes's arm. The paving stones bloomed with red patches like spilled wine. But at least they were still alive.

'Stop!' I cried.

Someone screamed, but not at me. No one even looked at me. They looked at Lady Anna, who was still screaming, then at the queen. Slowly, like a ship's sail collapsing as the wind died, the queen toppled from her chair.

Lady Hilda ran to her, and began to fan her. The queen murmured something, too soft for me to hear. Lady Annika pulled out smelling salts. For a moment I saw the queen stretched upon the ground, then she was lost in a froth of black skirts.

What was wrong? Surely she had not fainted at the sight of Hamlet's tiny wound? Queen Gertrude had seen bloodier sport. She had seen her son kill my father. She had not fainted then.

I ran forward, still unnoticed in the crowd, and tried to get closer. The lord of the exchequer shoved me back.

'Mind your manners, lout,' he snapped.

He had not recognised me. And this was not the time to pull off my hat and make myself known. The queen's face was blue. I had seen a face like that before — the dead king's. My blood turned to ice, as if the poison had me in its clutches too. Someone had poisoned the queen. Who? Why?

King Claudius had used poison before. I could see why he might poison Hamlet, or Laertes — no need for messy executions. But why kill his queen?

'Come again!' cried Hamlet, his back to his dying mother. He lunged at Laertes, turning as he did so. He stepped back, staring at his mother on the ground.

'How does the queen?' he panted.

The king's hands clutched the arms of his chair. He waved at Hamlet and Laertes to keep fighting. 'She swoons to see you bleed.'

Couldn't the king see his wife was dying? Hadn't he too seen that poisoned blue face?

I could do nothing for the queen that Lady Annika was not doing. Nothing but save her son. I must get between Hamlet and Laertes. Grab one of their rapiers before they began to fight again.

Laertes lifted his sword to strike at Hamlet.

'No!' The queen struggled up, cradled in Lady Annika's arms. 'No!' she cried weakly. 'No, the drink! The drink!' She struggled on her knees towards her son, her arms outstretched. 'Hamlet!'

'Mother?' It was the first time I had heard Hamlet use

the name. His rapier dropped onto the blood-splattered paving stones.

I ran to it, and grabbed it up.

'Laertes!' I cried.

My brother did not notice me. Did not hear me. Who listened to a servant? All his attention was on Hamlet, kneeling by the queen.

I wanted to go to her, but I was no lady-in-waiting now. I found tears in my eyes; the tears I should have shed for my wounded brother, my wounded lover. I watched as the queen laboured for breath, as her heart failed her; that valiant heart that had tried to do so much for Denmark.

'Oh, my dear Hamlet.' The words were as faint as a sparrow's breath.

She slumped against Lady Annika, a strange blue line about her mouth, even darker than the colour of her face. She seemed to force her eyes to open. One weak hand gestured at the table, where the goblets of wine still sat.

'I am poisoned!' she whispered harshly.

I looked at the goblets. The queen had offered Hamlet a drink, then had drunk from the cup herself. A poisoned chalice King Claudius meant for Hamlet.

The queen fell back. Lady Annika bent and closed her mistress's eyes. She stayed on the ground, her arms about the queen, while Lady Anna and Lady Hilda stood like guards on either side.

Hamlet stared at his mother's corpse. I waited for him to bend his head and weep. Instead, he surged to his feet.

'Oh, villainy! Lock the gate!' he cried, gesturing at the door to the palace. 'Treachery! Find out who did it!'

The king stared at his dead wife, then looked back at Hamlet. For a moment I thought the king might countermand the order, and stride away into the palace. Instead, he sat back, as if waiting. But for what? Surely he did not expect the duel to continue now? A strange smile flitted about his face. Still he waited, motionless. The whole court seemed frozen about him.

What was the king waiting for? Even I did not move, staring at him, then at Laertes, still holding his rapier, and at Hamlet, who once again seemed lost.

Suddenly Laertes fell to the ground, landing hard upon his knees, his head striking the grass.

'Laertes!' I dropped the rapier and ran to him, kneeled on the stones, parted his shirt to look at his wound. It oozed a little, but was not severe enough to cause him to faint. The skin around the wound was a faint, shiny blue. I gazed at his face in fear. He had not drunk the wine, had he? Surely he could not be poisoned too?

'Laertes,' I said. 'It is I!'

People screamed, shouted, shrieked around us. A chorus of cries, as if crows were trying to sing hymns. I did not think Laertes even heard me.

I lifted my brother. Suddenly I was shoved aside, so hard I fell against the paving stones, the wind knocked out of me. Hamlet took Laertes in his arms. I forced my body up, dragged in a breath.

'Hamlet!' It came out as a strangled whisper. 'Laertes!'

I tried again. I clambered to my knees, tried to crawl to them.

Another hand pushed me aside. Horatio. He kneeled by Hamlet, who was still holding my brother.

Laertes looked at Hamlet, not at me. He heaved a breath, then nodded towards the rapier I had dropped, the rapier he had fought with at the start of the duel.

'Treachery is here!' he whispered. 'Hamlet, you are dead.' The words were as weak as chicken feathers scratching paper. 'The treacherous rapier in your hand is poisoned.' Laertes forced a smile, a warrior's smile, acknowledging the ultimate defeat. 'My own poison has turned on me.'

'Laertes,' I whispered. But I didn't try to reach him now. My brother had more in common with Hamlet than with me. Warrior cradled warrior. I was just a girl. A girl who had done nothing. Who had not even saved her brother, much less her country.

'I can ... I can no more.' Laertes sank back. His voice rose in one last despairing whisper. 'The king! The king is to blame!'

And then my brother died.

The wind carried his words, soft as they were, through the garden. I sensed the moment they struck each lord and lady of the court, the guards and servants watching from the towers above.

Hamlet cradled my dead brother for a heartbeat more, then laid him gently on the grass. I crawled over to my brother. No one stopped me now. Perhaps they took me for my brother's servant, anguished at his loss. Besides, all watched Hamlet now.

I cradled my brother's corpse as Hamlet rose, his gaze on the king. One step, another. Hamlet drew back his rapier.

'The point poisoned?' Hamlet's voice was a hawk's croak, harsh and high. 'Then poison, do your work!'

He thrust the rapier at the king's heart. The watchers around me gasped; then gasped again as the narrow blade buckled on the king's thick doublet. Claudius was wearing leather, or even mail underneath, I thought. He was prepared for exactly this.

'Defend me, friends!' the king shouted. 'I am but hurt!'

Someone screamed.

Another called, 'Treason!' but without conviction.

No one stepped to help the king.

Lady Annika stood, then Lady Anna and Lady Hilda: three avenging angels next to the body of their mistress. They stared at the king, implacable. I had never known the three old women could look like this. Even their gazes could shred glass.

The king's guards glanced at them, then looked at the slain queen, and then at Laertes, limp in my arms. Then they too stared at the king.

The king stood up slowly. Was he still the king now no one would obey him? He stared around the garden, as if daring each courtier to move. He gazed at Hamlet again, then back at the court, as if hoping someone might throw him a sword.

No one moved.

Hamlet grabbed the poisoned goblet. 'Here, you incestuous, murderous Dane. Drink your potion! Then follow my mother.'

He seized the king's collar, as if he were a hound, and forced him down till he knelt upon the grass. The king opened his mouth as if to command his guards to strike — too late. The poisoned wine frothed red about his lips as Hamlet poured it down his throat.

Claudius stared at Hamlet, gulping and retching. He reached out once more towards his court. They stood there as still as the stones in the graveyard, each man, each woman, watching silently as the king's fingers grew limp.

The king collapsed, a small heap of old man and black velvet on the ground. Still no one went to him.

Lady Anna and Lady Hilda bent again to their dear queen. Lady Annika gestured to a footman to help them carry her.

My chest hurt. I had forgotten to breathe. I forced myself to take in air.

Laertes moved in my arms. Not dead! I whispered his name, hope ripping through me. It was so small a wound. Perhaps there was too little poison in it to kill him. Please, let my brother live …

'Hamlet?' Laertes's voice was a strangled gasp.

Hamlet ran to us and knelt on the grass. I could smell his breath, his sweat, and feel my brother's cooling warmth, yet I seemed as invisible to them as if I truly lay in the graveyard. Who looked at the face of a servant boy? Who noticed his tears?

Laertes reached out a trembling hand. 'Exchange forgiveness with me, noble Hamlet. You are not responsible for my death, nor my father's. Nor am I responsible for yours.'

His eyes widened as Hamlet's hand joined his. For a moment I thought, hoped, that the poison had bled itself from him. But then his body dropped, as if death weighed more than all his life. His frozen eyes gazed at the sky, not at his sister.

'Heaven make you free of it,' said Hamlet softly. He smiled, a strange smile, almost of relief. 'I follow you.' He looked up at his friend. 'I am dead, Horatio,' he said quietly.

He stood, walked two paces, staggered.

Horatio caught him and lowered him to the ground. The court stared, as if this were a play. The final act, I thought numbly, still cradling my dead brother.

Hamlet looked around the silent audience. 'You that look pale and tremble at this chance,' he whispered, 'oh, I could tell you ...' His voice faltered. 'Oh, but let it be. Horatio, I am dead. You live. You tell my story, and tell it right.'

'No!' Horatio gazed at Hamlet fiercely, then grabbed the poisoned goblet. 'I am more antique Roman than a Dane. There's some liquor left.'

Hamlet still wore that strange smile. At last, he was king of Denmark. He lay on the ground, curled a little, still smiling, like a child who longs for sleep and knows the longed-for rest has come.

'Give me the cup,' he whispered. 'Oh, good Horatio, I leave a wounded name. If you ever loved me, do this for me. Hold yourself away from happy death, just for a while. Stay in this harsh world to tell my story.'

Thunder growled over the forest. I looked up, startled. The sky was clear. There were no tears of rain, like the tears shed here.

The sound came again. Not thunder. Cannon.

'Young Fortinbras!' shouted someone. 'He is come from Poland!'

Hamlet raised himself on one elbow. Horatio helped him, and the lord of the exchequer, and then more lords, at last acknowledging their king.

'Tell Fortinbras he had my dying voice. Tell him ...' He smiled up at Horatio. Not at me. No, not at me. 'Tell him the rest is silence.'

The lord of the exchequer took Claudius's crown and laid it by Hamlet's head. The other lords stood, heads bowed at the young man who was king now only with his death. I sat there holding my brother in my arms, both of us forgotten.

So much lost for one small crown, I thought. A dead queen, two dead kings and a dead brother lying on the grass — murder, treason, love and hatred, all played out in a garden.

I laid my brother down. I could not claim him now. All I could give him, and my father, was the good name of our house. To do that the boy must vanish. I stood, my knees like butter.

Horatio still sat by Hamlet. He bent and kissed the pale blue cheek. 'Now cracks a noble heart,' he said softly. 'Goodnight, sweet prince, and flights of angels sing thee to thy rest.'

Goodnight, I thought. The rest, indeed, was silence.

Chapter 26

I stumbled from the garden, through the crowd of watching servants, along the palace's deserted corridors.

They were all gone: my father, my brother, my lover. The queen who had loved me, as I had truly loved her at the last. The prince who had loved me too, in his poor mad fashion. The brother who had loved the idea of a sister more than the girl I was; who had never really seen me, even when I held his dying body. The king who might have killed me. All gone.

My heart should have been ripped from me. I felt it, and found that it was still there, beating. I was here, even if they had vanished into the realm of death.

And what was left? Fortinbras and his army, at our gates. Ophelia: no man's daughter and no man's sister now. My family's estates would be inherited by a distant cousin, not by a girl. All around me seemed grey, as if the clouds had eaten Denmark.

Doubt thou the stars are fire ...

I had loved him, but I could not mourn him. Denmark was safer for his loss.

I had lost my own life with those corpses in the garden. No brother to protect me; no lover to comfort me; no queen to order my days. It wasn't even safe for me to flee to our estates and wait to see if the cousin who inherited them would give me a home. No girl would be safe travelling through the countryside with Fortinbras's army in our land.

'Oh, ghosts,' I whispered, 'tell me what I should do.'

But no ghost fluttered towards me, not the ghost of father, brother, king. Ghosts could not come by day. They had no message for me. Nothing.

And that, I thought, is what my life is now. Nothing. I had no place to flee to, neither as a girl, nor as the boy I appeared to be. Ophelia was like the flowers strewn upon the ground, her future as soon faded. I glanced down at my shirt and breeches.

But I was not Ophelia now, I realised; Ophelia was in the grave in the churchyard. She could stay there. What use was she now? Horatio would see my brother buried. And poor Hamlet had no need of me, nor the queen. In my trousers I was …

I felt a smile, faint as a breeze across my face. Sir Roderick, I thought. No, perhaps not sir, for then I would have to explain where my estate was. Nor was I dressed fine enough to be a knight.

Slowly, colour seeped back into my world. Safer to be

William the Smith's son. Bill Smithson, orphaned by ... by the plague. And how did Bill Smithson live?

I did smile then, as a path opened up before me, like a trail between nettles. Bill Smithson could live well. My mother's jewels were hidden behind her portrait in my bedroom: strings of pearls and rubies, a tiara and an emerald brooch. Jewels could be carried in one's purse. No, they would be safer wrapped in a stocking and tied about my body. I could sell the stones one by one. And I had money too. I suspected my housekeeping allowance would buy me passage to anywhere in Europe.

I would have to travel on foot at first, hiding from other travellers. But it was summer: I could hide between the trees, sleep in my cloak at night. And when I was far enough away from Elsinore, I could take a coach to ... where?

I smiled. It seemed so right. To Wittenberg, of course.

Bill Smithson had been brought up to fashion iron into many shapes, but he had a heart that loved learning. He would hire a tutor at Wittenberg, learn Greek and Latin till he had enough to go to the university. And then he would have the entire universe to study.

One pearl sold every year might give me a cottage. A servant whom I could trust, because betraying me would mean losing their employment. And one day, perhaps, Bill Smithson might vanish, and a widow appear, who might love a man and marry him — if he let her keep her books.

I had a future now.

I began to run, up the stairs, and along the corridor to the door that led to our house.

The door was shut. No guard stood beside it. I opened it, listened. All was quiet — in our house as well as in the palace. I had seen no one on my way here. The whole palace was grieving; or, perhaps, gathering the silver before Fortinbras's soldiers stole it.

I walked to my room unseen, shut the door and reached for the key hidden behind a tapestry. I pushed aside the portrait of my mother, which hid the safe that held the jewels. I opened the door and pulled out the jewel box.

Now for stockings, to hide the treasure about my waist.

'Ophelia?'

I started and turned. Lady Annika stood at the door, her usually sleepy eyes as sharp and penetrating as sapphires. She must have come here straight from the garden.

I bowed, and made my voice gruff. 'My pardon, lady, I have the wrong apartment. I bid you adieu —'

'My dear, you have been wearing those ... garments for five years or more. Did you think we didn't know?' She added sharply, 'I hope you have not cut off your hair.'

I stared at her, stunned, then pulled my cap off automatically and let my hair tumble down. 'Not yet.'

'Good, for we have need of it.'

'Madam, I do not understand.' Who was this woman with a familiar face but a voice of steel?

'There is an army at our door. And chaos, if we do not deal with it. Here, sit. Now put your skirts back on.'

She blew her whistle to call the servants. I heard feet running up the stairs, then along the corridor.

Lady Annika went to the door to stop Gerda from looking in. 'A posset for the Lady Ophelia. And one for me.'

I hadn't realised I was hungry until I heard the words. I hadn't eaten since the night before.

'But, my lady, Lady Ophelia is dead,' said Gerda's tear-hoarse voice.

'A mistake. A farm girl, sadly drowned instead.'

'She is alive! Oh, madam —'

'And hungry. Hurry!' Lady Annika shut the door and turned to me. 'Denmark needs a queen.'

'The queen is dead,' I said stupidly.

'I know,' Lady Annika's voice was dry, 'I was there. I was there when she was made queen too, at both her marriages. Poor Gertrude did her best, but now we need another. Young Fortinbras will be heading for the throne room. We do not want him to find it empty. Quickly, into your skirts. No, into your nightdress first, so the servants may see you in it. We will say you have been ill, delirious with a fever. That should stop all talk of madness too. Though it was a good show you put on, girl.' She smiled at me. 'I pretended to be mad once, when my father wanted to marry me to a brute. It worked too. Well, we women must use the weapons we have to hand.'

She moved to the chest where my nightdresses were kept, leaving the way to the door clear. Should I run with the jewels now? The roads would not be safe, but I might hide on a fishing boat. Surely there would be many captains sailing with the tide, to keep their ships safe during the invasion. I could be safe in Wittenberg by next week. What did I want with more plotting, this time by a sleepy crone?

Yet she did not look sleepy now. Nor as old as I'd once thought her. I stared at her. Hamlet had tried to hide in madness. Could age and infirmity be a disguise too?

'The servants will know I haven't been here,' I said.

Lady Annika looked up from the chest. 'The servants will gossip, as they always do. But a girl lying in her bed, delirious and fevered after the death of her father, is more believable than a young lady faking her own death, then hiding in man's clothing up a tower.'

'You knew I went there?'

'For years, my dear. You are not the only one who can't sleep at night.'

I shook my head to clear it. Lady Annika was right: I did need food.

Her dried-apple face softened. 'My dear, I recognised you in the garden too. Do not worry, I am sure no one else did. There was too much else to look at.'

I nodded numbly, remembering our dead queen, Hamlet, my brother.

'I loved her too,' said Lady Annika quietly. 'Such a sweet girl she was. And courageous. No matter what that brute did, she bore it and kept smiling. Ah, a smile can be a weapon too.'

I nodded mutely.

'I loved Hamlet as well,' said Lady Annika.

I stared at her, startled.

'He was such a pretty baby, all curls and gurgles. I remember the day his father ordered the curls cut off. His son should not look soft and girl-like. Hamlet cried. Not for the curls, but because he did not have his father's love. He would never have it, for his father did not have any to give. Oh, yes, my dear, I have seen a lot, and loved too. And lost much that I loved. But not all of it.' Her eyes met mine. 'My life is not over yet. Neither is yours. We both still have worlds to conquer, if you have the stomach for it.'

I said nothing. Had no words to say.

'Well? Gertrude said you had the stomach of a queen. Was she wrong?'

And suddenly words came, and courage too. 'No,' I said. 'She was not wrong.'

I felt my ghosts smile at my answer. I was not alone. If ghosts could walk the earth for vengeance, surely they could walk it for good too. I could feel Father near me, as surely as if he stood there making a speech. King Fortinbras as well, nodding. And the shade of Queen Gertrude, there to support me as I had once supported her.

The door opened. Gerda came in, with the kitchen maid and a laden tray, peering at me with hope and joy.

'Put it down. We will help ourselves,' said Lady Annika.

She handed me a goblet of posset. I clutched at its warmth, despite the sunny day, and sipped. Cream and brandy, eggs and nutmeg. I found my hands were shaking. I'd had enough of weeping, but tears came nonetheless.

Lady Annika watched me calmly. 'For whom do you weep?'

Was it for Laertes? I asked myself. Or for poor Hamlet, who had loved me, but perhaps not as much as he had claimed?

'I weep for Denmark,' I whispered. 'Who shall care for her now?'

'Young Fortinbras may do quite well,' Lady Annika said. 'We've had good reports of him. He even seems to be keeping his army under control, which is harder, I believe, than persuading it to win. But Denmark needs a queen. She has needed one for many years, but old King Hamlet would never have one sitting by his side. He had to go, of course,' she added, 'with young Fortinbras ready to tear him off the throne. It is a pity that when Gertrude finally had a throne, her reign was cut so short.'

I looked at Lady Annika, peering serenely at me from between her wrinkles. How much of the plot to kill King Hamlet did you know? I wondered. Did you and Gertrude plan it together; perhaps not all, but some? Did she smile at Claudius, knowing it would inflame him enough to kill his brother? What was this old woman planning now?

'You said we need a queen,' I said slowly.

'We do. Young Fortinbras has no wife.'

'And you would give me to him?'

'I would give him myself, gladly,' she said frankly, 'were I fifty years younger.' She smiled, and I saw in it the rags left of her beauty. 'Or even thirty years, perhaps. But you must net him now.'

'How, madam?' And then I knew.

She saw it in my face. 'Well done, girl. We will advise you, of course.'

'We?'

'The ladies of your court. Did you think we were there only to sew tapestries?'

She clapped her hands. The maids must have been listening outside the door for they opened it at once.

'The gold dress hanging in my chambers — bring it here,' she told them. She looked at me again. 'And we must do something with your hair.'

Chapter 27

They dressed me, the three women — Lady Annika, Lady Hilda and Lady Anna — in a green silk petticoat with an overskirt of gold, gold sleeves and a green kirtle. They brushed my hair and left it hanging loose, my head crowned with ropes of pearls and roses.

The maids brought me a mirror. I saw summer in my reflection — the harvest of ripe wheat; the lush green grass and green trees; and yellow cheeses, the land's wealth. Denmark needs a queen, I thought, who knows why cheese is so important. Swords are all very well, as long as you have a store of cheese.

The three ladies-in-waiting walked behind me across the courtyard to the throne room. My ghosts came too. I could not see them — might never see them, even at midnight in my tower — but I knew they were with me still.

The porter stared at me as we entered the great hall. 'But, my lady,' he said stupidly, 'what about your grave?'

'It will keep,' I said. 'For another sixty years or so.

Please tell Prince Fortinbras that I am waiting for him in the throne room. And tell the lord of the exchequer too.'

Fortinbras's army had swords, but the exchequer had the money.

The porter bowed. Not a servant's bob, but a deep one, to the floor.

I smiled, and felt the warmth of approval like a small sun on my back from the ladies who walked behind me.

I looked out the open doors and up at my small tower. Old King Hamlet would not walk there again, I realised, even in the darkest winter midnight. He had been avenged, even if his son had died doing it.

Old King Fortinbras had been avenged too. His usurper had been killed, along with the usurper's brother and wife and son. But I didn't think my ghost would leave Elsinore, not yet. He would want to see his son live a good and happy life, and his grandchildren too.

I remembered something else King Fortinbras had said: 'Hate begets hate.' We had seen that in Denmark this past year. Brother killing brother; father urging son to kill again. All who had hated, who had plotted, were now dead; the entire House of Hamlet was gone, as if the snows had frozen it forever.

Good men had died too. My father and my brother.

It was time for a new rule now. Kindness instead of hate. Compassion for our people. No shadows, no vengeance from the past. Just good sense, and cheese.

'You would be a good queen,' the ghost had told me when I was a child. I knew how to be one now.

'Thank you,' I whispered to my ghosts: my sensible father, clever queen, the wise dead king. But there was no wind, not even a breeze, to answer.

We walked on, into the throne room. The two thrones were still arranged side by side. Gertrude's was warm, as if she had only just left it. You taught me the game well, I thought. But a hive can only have one queen.

My stomach growled. I should have had more than just the posset. I wanted breakfast, or even dinner, but it would spoil the regal image if the prince arrived to find me munching on pickled herring.

The old women arranged themselves below the dais, sitting on the stools at my feet.

The doors opened. Two knights came in, then stood on each side of the doors. I waited for the trumpets to sound. But this young man had no need of trumpets. He stood there, in the doorway. He must have changed from his travel-stained clothes, for he wore silver velvet.

I smiled. Gold and silver. We matched well.

He was younger than I'd thought he would be; a year younger, perhaps, than poor Hamlet. Neither tall nor short, but sturdy; a man used to sword play, to riding with his men. A man who had turned aside from conquering Denmark. Who had, when it had come to it, put aside revenge. He had a look about him of his father. I hoped he had his father's kindness and wisdom too.

He scrutinised me before he spoke. 'I had thought to find the throne of Denmark empty.'

I smiled. 'There are two thrones here, my lord, a king's and a queen's. And one of them is empty.' I stood. 'I am Ophelia, daughter of our late chancellor, lord of Denmark's largest estates, and betrothed of the late Prince Hamlet, the girl who all expected would be queen.'

It was an invitation and a warning. Lord Fortinbras grinned. He understood them both.

He gestured to his men, to the servants peering in at the door. 'Away!' He inspected Lady Annika, Lady Hilda and Lady Anna, and bowed low. 'If your gentlenesses would excuse us for a time alone?'

The old ladies rose. As one they curtseyed deeply, as to a king, and then to me, equally deeply, as to a queen.

'But, sir!' One of his guardsmen lingered. 'Is it wise to be alone in such a place?'

'Do you think this lady will stab me with a fruit knife?'

The guard looked at me warily, as if he thought I was capable of exactly that. 'No, sir.'

'Then go. I expect she and I will deal well together.'

They left. He walked towards me.

I held out my hand. 'I bid you welcome to Elsinore, Lord Fortinbras.'

He bowed and kissed my hand. 'Well, my lady?'

'Very well indeed,' I said, and sat on the throne again. It was as if I had always sat there now. 'Denmark needs a king. It seems we may have found one.'

He looked amused. 'You have.'

'A sensible king. A man who knows what to do and when to do it. A man whom the people will accept.'

He was enjoying this. 'Why will they accept him, madam?'

'Because he has arrived with an army of great might, which probably has a mighty thirst. I warrant your men are already filling all the alehouses.'

He raised an eyebrow. The grin appeared again. 'I thought that perhaps you meant because he will marry the Princess Ophelia.'

'That too, of course. But I have never been a princess. Only a girl who would be queen.'

'Yes, we will deal well together,' he repeated. 'May I take the throne beside you, madam?'

'Of course, my lord. And then perhaps we might call the court in to greet us properly.' I raised an eyebrow of my own. 'And the captains of your army, before they are too drunk to stand.'

'And you can show me where the garderobes are, and other useful things. But first ...'

He bent and kissed me again, first on the back of my hand, and then on my mouth. His lips were warm. He smelled of man.

I thought: why didn't Hamlet kiss me like this? And then I didn't think at all.

Some time later he raised his head and grinned at me again. 'Now we will call in the court.'

He sat on the king's throne. I watched him arrange his face, a king now, not a lover. I chose my expression too. He lifted his hand and hit the gong to call the others in, then reached for my hand and held it tightly.

The doors opened. His men jostled briefly with the lord of the exchequer. The lord of the exchequer won by a grey whisker. He made his way towards us, Lord Fortinbras's men behind him, then the courtiers, and, at the back, my ladies of the bedchamber, looking again as if they had no thoughts beyond their tapestries.

You sew well, my ladies, I thought, and not just cloth.

The lord of the exchequer bowed low. 'What is your wish, my lady, my lord?'

He was no fool, the lord of the exchequer. No fool at all. Our new lord chancellor, perhaps? Fortinbras and I must discuss this further, when we were alone.

Fortinbras was already speaking. 'The archbishop, to marry us. At once, if you please.' He turned to me. 'You have no objection, Lady Ophelia?'

I should be grieving, I thought. A year in mourning for my father, my brother, for Hamlet. But Denmark could not spare me a year. Nor did I want it. And I had the example of Queen Gertrude, who had not let mourning stop her placing this throne here, on which I now sat.

'No, my lord,' I said demurely. 'It shall be exactly as you wish.'

He grinned. 'Somehow I doubt it.' He turned back to the lord of the exchequer. 'A quick anointing afterwards. Nothing elaborate. We can leave the coronation proper for next week.'

'And dinner,' I added. 'Now.'

'Certainly.' The lord of the exchequer hailed a servant. 'Bring venison, pastries, roast goose ...'

I sighed. The palace cooks would not have begun dinner with their royal masters dead. It takes hours to roast a goose.

'Bread and cheese will do me,' said Fortinbras. He raised his eyebrow at me, half apologetically. 'Soldier's fare, but none the worse for it.'

'As long as it is good cheese,' I informed him.

He laughed. How long had it been since these walls had heard laughter? 'Of course, madam. It must be good cheese.'

'Bread and cheese,' I told the lord of the exchequer sweetly. 'Midsummer Gold, three years old, and well-cellared. Barley, rye or wheat bread, whichever is freshest. And fast, if you please.' I turned back to Fortinbras, his hand still warm in mine. 'We must show ourselves to the people, my lord, on the balcony above the square.'

That would help keep his troops in line too, I thought. Remind them that this was no town they had conquered, to be sacked, but a kingdom where they would live in peace, with plenty of cheese and herring.

'A balcony scene,' said Fortinbras. 'I like that. I suspect the crowd will too.'

The servants were already carrying in trays holding flagons of wine and ale, loaves of fresh rye bread and cheeses: caraway and green cheese, double cream and Musty Maude, Queen's Blue and, at the front, a hunk of Midsummer Gold. I glanced at Lady Annika. Exactly three years old, I had no doubt. A perfect cheese.

'I hope the goblets have been washed well,' I said. We didn't need the remnants of Claudius's poison now.

'Of course,' said Lady Annika.

Her eyes were almost closed again, but a half-smile lingered under her bristly top lip. Lady Hilda and Lady Anna picked up their tapestries.

'With your permission, Your Majesties?' The lord of the exchequer took a gleamingly clean goblet filled with wine that was definitely not poisoned, and raised it up. 'I give to you all a toast. To King Fortinbras, and to Ophelia, queen of Denmark.'

I held my prince's hand and smiled. I felt his warmth, the heat of the old stones of the palace, the sun that shone on the lush grass of Denmark that would give us a harvest of good cheese.

I felt my ghosts smile too.

Author's Notes

First, my apologies to Denmark, its royalty and its history. This book isn't set in Denmark, or any other country; rather the setting is a blend of my imagination and Shakespeare's, who set his plays in the worlds within his mind. Any glimpses of the real Denmark are a gift from a dear friend, Linda Bunn, and her stories shared about her childhood there.

This story wriggles between the lines of Shakespeare's play *The Tragedy of Hamlet, Prince of Denmark*. There is nothing in it that contradicts the play, but there is much that certainly isn't what Shakespeare intended. This isn't his play fleshed out — as in my book *I am Juliet* — but another story twisted into his.

Would Shakespeare have minded? Probably he would have been justly annoyed that I wasn't able to do him the courtesy of asking his permission, though his ghost did not appear on our veranda to condemn me while I was writing this book. Shakespeare has no direct descendants to inherit his play that I could have asked — except, of course, his audiences over the centuries.

Shakespeare certainly suffered from plagiarists stealing his plays while he was still alive, including whoever published the First Quarto (so called because the printing sheets were folded), which contains the first known and poorest version of *Hamlet*. Possibly it was stolen by someone who'd been to see the play, or even dictated by one of the actors who no longer had the script to copy.

But if I had been able to ask Shakespeare's permission to rewrite his play, I suspect he may have given it to me. Shakespeare too took other people's work and changed it to become his own. He was also a theatre manager as well as a playwright, in the days when each performance of the play might differ from another to fit the abilities of the available cast, or the appetites and moods of the audience. A brilliant actor might be given a larger part; an apprentice actor might have his part reduced. A performance for Queen Elizabeth I or King James I might have differed considerably from that presented to an audience of farmers and labourers. Or perhaps not. Without seeing Shakespeare's original scripts, we cannot know. But I do not feel the weight of his anger sitting on my shoulder, muttering, 'What have you done to my play, old crone? And to placate my impertinent curiosity, what clothes are those upon your nether limbs?'

Ours is a world where women wear jeans, and Shakespeare's plays are studied on the page, not experienced on the stage. I suspect Shakespeare would be more horrified by his plays being studied in books than with the liberties I've taken with his plot and script.

Shakespeare's plays, even a tragedy like *Hamlet*, were full of movement and laughter. On stage, the actors could break up long speeches with movement and expression, or a bit of 'business', like playing with a dancing bear. (A dancing bear performed just down from The Globe, Shakespeare's theatre, and seems to have been added whenever a play threatened to become a little long-winded or tedious.) Gorgeous costumes helped too — often donated second-hand, when Shakespeare's patrons were tired of them or they were moth-eaten; as did music, sword fights, love-making, and coarse jokes that modern audiences no longer notice because the English language has changed so much.

Hamlet is perhaps the most perfect of black comedies, but unless you are used to the language, it doesn't read like that. Language in Shakespeare's time was more formal, florid and wordy than it is now. Shakespeare's work wasn't intended for the uneducated. It cost at least a penny to see a play; more often threepence if you wanted to sit on a stool. At a time when a journeyman or tutor might get thirty shillings a year, this was a high price to pay to see a play. You could enjoy a hanging for free.

Those of breeding and education (Shakespeare was a glove-maker's son but he was well-educated) prided themselves on witty speech, flights of impromptu poetry and wordplay. The quotes attributed to Queen

Elizabeth I show an ease and playfulness with words; and while those that have survived are undoubtedly among the wittiest, they're evidence that the classes who attended Shakespeare's plays were used to language more elaborate than we are today. Even in my lifetime, our speech and writing styles have become shorter and plainer — an effect of TV, texting, emails and, possibly, a faster, more impatient pace of life. These days it is rare to hear the long embroidered anecdotes of my childhood, when every adult was happy to tell you at great length over dinner or an afternoon biscuit long stories about their childhood, the war, or encounters with a bunyip.

MELODRAMA

Shakespeare's world was naturally melodramatic. A third of a village might die of plague within a week. Traitors were tortured and publicly beheaded. Young men fought with rapiers in the streets. A man might have three wives, who died one after the other in childbirth. The wrong religion might result in you being tortured or burned at the stake. Children were taken to see men hanged or traitors' heads rotting on stakes in the same way they might be taken to an amusement park now. Mary Queen of Scots' supporters' plots against her cousin, Queen Elizabeth I, were as dramatic, and unlikely, as anything in *Hamlet*.

In our, more sensible age, Ophelia would have talked everything over with her best friends; Hamlet would have seen a grief counsellor. When Polonius died, Ophelia would have sent a text to Laertes to tell him, and discuss what to do next. Mobile phones would have wrecked the plots of most of Shakespeare's plays.

Shakespeare probably chose to start *Hamlet* with the king's ghost appearing on the battlements because it makes for a rattling good dramatic performance. There is a legend that Shakespeare himself played the part of the ghost. I imagine he played it wonderfully.

THE HISTORY OF THE PLAY

The Tragedy of Hamlet, Prince of Denmark was written and first performed about 1599–1600. Noted Elizabethan actor Richard Burbage made the title role famous.

The play wasn't published then; Shakespeare would have wanted to keep it for his own company of players. He would have kept all his handwritten copies locked away, and shown them only to the actors so they could learn their parts.

The pirated First Quarto appeared in 1603 or 1604.

Hamlet was published with other plays by Shakespeare in 1632, after his death. This version is known as the First Folio — another printing term.

Why did Shakespeare set the play in Denmark? James I, the new king of England, had a Danish wife, so the play might have been meant as a compliment to her; and to the king, by showing a usurping royal house being overthrown and the true heir of Denmark returning to its throne.

Shakespeare's own son was named Hamnet, but I doubt it was in honour of the play. The play's Hamlet isn't really a role model for any young man. Maybe Shakespeare just liked the name.

Was there a real Hamlet? Possibly. Maybe. Unlikely. And only a small resemblance, if there was.

A sixteen-book collection of Norse legends, *Gesta Danorum*, or *History of the Danes*, collected by Saxo Grammaticus and written in Latin around 1200 AD, includes the possibly true story of a man called Amleth, son of one of two brothers who were joint kings of Jutland. Amleth pretended to be mad after his uncle killed his father and married his mother. His pretence of madness worked: he avenged his father and became king of Jutland.

The *Gesta Danorum* books were published in Paris in 1514. In 1570, Francois de Belleforest translated them into French and included them in a collection of tragic stories called *Histoires Tragiques*.

In 1608, a story appeared in English called *The Hystorie of Hamblet*. It might have been a translation of de Belleforest's work, or a story based on Shakespeare's play, or a combination of both. The Amleth, Hamblet and Hamlet stories differ in major ways.

There are also references to a play called *Hamlet* by Thomas Kyd, written in the 1580s, in which a ghostly father cries, 'Hamlet, revenge.' But no copies of that play seem to have survived, only accounts from theatre-goers who saw it, so there is no way of knowing how much Shakespeare's version copied Kyd's, or even if Shakespeare's company took Kyd's play and gradually improved it.

It's also possible that the First Quarto version of *Hamlet* might be a combination of Kyd's work and Shakespeare's, or a draft from the time when Shakespeare was turning Kyd's work into the play we now know. But this is only conjecture, building theories with few facts.

No matter how many similarities there are between the various adaptations of the central story, it is indisputable that it was Shakespeare's work that became an instant hit, and has remained so through all the centuries since it was first played. Even when the theatres were closed by the Puritans in Cromwell's England between 1642 and 1660, versions of *Hamlet* were still performed in taverns and inns. And it was one of the first great theatrical successes once the theatres were allowed to open again.

CHEESE

The cheeses in this book are only as real as the characters and places; in other words, I have made them up. But they do obey the rules of real cheeses made from cow's, sheep's or goat's milk, with thousands of permutations depending on the season, what sort of grass or other fodder the animals have eaten, how the cheeses have been made and stored or aged, and what other ingredients have been added. As my Ophelia would well know, a cheese from the same cow's milk can vary enormously if made by a different person, or by the same person and using the same recipe but at a different time of year when the grass is drier or sweeter or more lush, or when the cow's offspring are very young, or later in their lactation when they are older.

In Shakespeare's time, every region, even most farmhouses, had their own particular cheeses, most of them known only as far away as the next village. They were often called after the women who made them, or who had invented them; or given picturesque names, like Wette Willie, to raise a smile in winter. The names would not have been recorded, which is why this book has its own cheeses, not the ones that are made today.

In cold climates, and before the days of refrigeration and canning, a household's survival depended on its stocks of salted or smoked meat, dried or smoked fish, dried fruits, sacks of flour, barrels of salted or fermented or clarified butter, and, most of all, cheese. Cheese was women's work, and women's wealth too. In many northern countries, if a woman was divorced by her husband, she took the household's cheeses with her when she left. Waxing, soaking in brine, rolling in dried leaves or wood ash, and the development of hard rinds were all ways to keep cheeses through the winter and early spring months, till the grass grew again, and the cows, sheep and goats gave birth and began producing milk once more. These kinds of cheeses are delicious, but they were born from desperation and the need to survive when snow covered the earth and nothing grew.

It's easy to make cheese. It's also easy to make a cheese that will last over winter. It's harder to make a good cheese, and even more difficult to make a superbly delicious one. If you wish to make cheese properly, buy a book on the subject, seek out the correct 'starters' and, if possible, do an apprenticeship with a good cheese-maker. More and more good artisan cheese-makers offer weekend workshops in cheese-making, and you can choose the types of cheeses you want to tackle first. But beware: cheese-making can become a totally absorbing hobby. Even your first attempts will probably be better than the 'rat trap' cheese sold in sweaty plastic in the supermarket.

WARNING: All cheese can contain listeria or bacteria or moulds that can give you food poisoning. Do not experiment with home-made cheese if you're pregnant, or have low immunity. Don't eat commercial soft cheeses either.

Fresh or 'green' cheese
Fresh or 'green' cheeses, such as cottage cheese and cream cheese, only take a few minutes to make. They're very adaptable — try them with fruit for lunch; on bread or biscuits; crumbled over steamed vegetables; or with a spoonful of jam and fresh cream for dessert.

Their flavour will vary with the season; as all food should vary, rather than being a year-long predictable harvest from the fridge.

Cottage cheese

This gets its name because it was so easily and quickly made in any cottage and needs no particular skill or equipment. Full cream milk is best, but a thinner cottage cheese can be made from most milks. Though if your first attempt is too thin and watery, try a better quality milk. (I have only made this with fresh cow's milk.)

Gently heat two litres of milk so it feels neither hot nor cold to your wrist. (Don't use your fingers to test the temperature as they may be calloused and so not as sensitive.) Add half a junket tablet (from the supermarket), or half a cup of lemon juice, or half a cup of puréed sour sorrel (the latter makes a bitter, pale green cheese). Cover the bowl and leave it in a warm place till the milk goes lumpy — about twenty-four hours or longer. Line a sieve or colander with a clean tea towel, pour in the lumpy milk and allow the whey (the clear runny residue of cheese-making) to drain off. This will take about another twenty-four hours. You'll be left with thick white curds — the cottage cheese. The cheese is now ready to eat.

You can add salt if you like, but cottage cheese is naturally quite salty. Chopped fresh herbs and freshly ground black pepper are a good addition.

Cream cheese

This cheese is very smooth and can be used instead of butter.

Simmer half a litre of cream for five minutes. Leave the cream to get cold, then whip it well. When it's thick, turn it into a clean tea towel and hang it overnight, or for two to three days and nights. The watery whey will drip out. Be careful — whey is sticky and messy. I usually hang ours over a shower or bath so the mess is easily washed away. Do not do this in hot weather, unless your bathroom is air-conditioned or very cool.

When you unwrap the cheese, it will be roundish and thick enough to slice, though it will crumble a bit.

Variations: I sometimes add four tablespoons of Cointreau, one tablespoon of grated orange zest and four tablespoons of caster sugar to the cream before whipping it. This makes a superb dessert — by itself, with raspberries, or with more fresh thick cream.

You can also add chopped walnuts, grated lemon zest, vanilla or orange or rosewater or kirsch.

Farmer's baked cheese

Whip two cups of cream cheese with one cup of thick fresh cream and three eggs. Add sugar and flavouring to taste: try the orange flavouring above, or a little vanilla, or add sour cream instead of sweet cream mixed with grated lemon zest.

Bake at 150 degrees Celsius for about an hour or two,

until firm. Eat hot or cold, with more cream, fruit and ice-cream.

Fresh-milk cheese

This isn't a cottage cheese or cream cheese; it's simply a fresh cheese made with milk and no cream, so it has a lower fat content.

Fill a bowl with milk, and leave it for two days at room temperature. (This assumes your room is a comfortable temperature. If it's very warm, keep the milk in a cool cupboard or pantry.) The milk should thicken slightly without going bad. You can hasten this process by adding a junket tablet, but there's no need if you have patience.

Pour the milk into a cloth — I use a clean tea towel, doubled over — and hang it in a cool place, like over the bath, till the liquid has run out and the cheese is firm.

Serve with fresh fruit, fresh fruit purée, cream or sugar.

Hard cheese

Take a large bowl of milk and leave it out overnight. Next morning, warm the milk to blood heat, so it feels neither hot nor cold to the inside of your wrist.

Stir the milk well, add a little rennet (an enzyme found in the lining of a calf's stomach, usually dried; available from the supermarket), or half a junket tablet, or a commercial cheese 'starter', which will give by far the best results. Stir, and leave it in a warm place till it sets like custard.

Cut the curd gently with a sharp knife into tiny squares, then keep slicing till they almost mix together again. Now heat slowly to 38 degrees Celsius (about blood heat), occasionally stirring gently. Try to keep the curds at this temperature for about an hour, either in the oven at its lowest possible heat, or at the side of a wood-burning stove, or wrapped in a blanket.

Now ladle the curds into a clean tea towel inside a sieve, so the watery whey can drain off. This may take a night or two.

Press the now firm curds into a round, wrap it in several tea towels pre-soaked in salt and water, and dry it.

Put the wrapped cheese on a wire tray or sieve, press it flat in its tea towels, then put a weight on top to force out even more moisture. This weight should be as heavy as you can manage — a couple of bricks covered in a clean tea towel are excellent.

After two hours, turn the cheese over and put the weight on the other side.

Repeat this turning process for at least a fortnight.

Unwrap your cheese. If it looks and smells good — not rotten or mouldy — coat it in a salt crust, wax or a combination of butter and melted paraffin. Leave it in a cool place for three months, and turn it every day.

This type of cheese can be eaten fresh, but it won't be ripe. I prefer cheese that's three weeks or so old — it's milder and soapier. Of course, you can leave the cheese for much longer than three months, and the taste will be stronger and richer.

A good cheese can be stored for years or decades and may get better with time, but you need to know how to turn it, store it and age it, as well as possibly covering it with wax or salt. Making a mature cheese is an art and a skill.

If you want a very yellow cheese, add a few calendula petals when first pressing.

Clotted cream

This is the cream that should accompany a Devonshire tea. It's far superior to whipped cream and lasts much longer, whether in the fridge or out of it.

Heat non-homogenised milk to just below boiling point — just too hot to touch. Leave overnight at room temperature, or near a heater in cold weather, in a covered bowl.

The next morning, skim off the cream. It will be almost thick enough to slice, a bit like solid silk. And delicious.

Clotted cream can be used with the methods above to make a superb cream cheese.

Try either clotted cream or cream cheese with fresh raspberries or strawberries, the small ones with flavour, that Shakespeare knew. The Ophelia of this book would not have approved of supermarket varieties.

Jackie French AM is an award-winning writer, wombat negotiator, the Australian Children's Laureate for 2014–2015 and the 2015 Senior Australian of the Year. She is regarded as one of Australia's most popular children's authors and writes across all genres — from picture books, history, fantasy, ecology and sci-fi to her much loved historical fiction. 'Share a Story' is the primary philosophy behind Jackie's two-year term as Laureate.

jackiefrench.com.au
facebook.com/authorjackiefrench